No Qu

FACE FROM THE PAST

THE CRIME SCENE CLUB: FACT AND FICTION

6

Skull Reconstruction

THE CRIME SCENE CLUB: FACT AND FICTION

FACE FROM THE PAST

Skull Reconstruction

Kenneth McIntosh

Mason Crest Publishers

FACE FROM THE PAST:
SKULL RECONSTRUCTION

MASON CREST PUBLISHERS INC.
370 Reed Road
Broomall, Pennsylvania 19008
(866)MCP-BOOK (toll free)
www.masoncrest.com

First Printing

9 8 7 6 5 4 3 2 1

ISBN 978-1-4222-0259-3 (series)
Library of Congress Cataloging-in-Publication Data

McIntosh, Kenneth, 1959–
  Face from the past : skull reconstruction / by Kenneth McIntosh.
    p. cm. — (The Crime Scene Club ; case #6)
  Includes bibliographical references.
  ISBN 978-1-4222-0252-4   ISBN 978-1-4222-1455-8
[1. Criminal investigation—Fiction. 2. Forensic sciences—Fiction. 3. Mystery and detective stories.] I. Title.
  PZ7.M1858Fac 2009
  [Fic]—dc22
                              2008033241

Design by MK Bassett-Harvey.
Produced by Harding House Publishing Service, Inc.
www.hardinghousepages.com
Cover design by MK Bassett-Harvey.
Cover and interior illustrations by Justin Miller.
Printed in Malaysia.

CONTENTS

INTRODUCTION

The sound of breaking glass. A scream. A shot. Then . . . silence. Blood, fingerprints, a bullet, a skull, fire debris, a hair, shoeprints—enter the wonderful world of forensic science. A world of searching to find clues, collecting that which others cannot see, testing to find answers to seemingly impossible questions, and testifying to juries so that justice will be served. A world where curiosity, love of a puzzle, and gathering information are basic. The books in this series will take you to this world.

The CSI Effect

The TV show *CSI: Crime Scene Investigator* became so widely popular that *CSI: Miami* and *CSI: NY* followed. This forensic interest spilled over into *Bones* (anthropology); *Crossing Jordan* and *Dr. G* (medical examiners); *New Detectives* and *Forensic Files*, which cover all the forensic disciplines. Almost every modern detective story now involves forensic science. Many fiction books are written, some by forensic scientists such as Kathy Reichs (anthropology) and Ken Goddard (criminalistics and crime scene), as well as textbooks such as *Criminalistics* by Richard Saferstein. Other crime fiction authors are Sir Arthur Conan Doyle (Sherlock Holmes), Thomas Harris (*Red Dragon*), Agatha Christie (Hercule Poirot) and Ellis Peters, whose hero is a monk, Cadfael, an ex-Crusader who solves crimes. The list goes on and on—and I encourage you to read them all!

The spotlight on forensic science has had good *and* bad effects, however. Because the books and TV shows are so enjoyable, the limits of science have been blurred to make the plots more interesting. Often when students are intrigued by the TV shows and want to learn more, they have a rude awakening. The crime scene investigators on TV do the work of many professionals, including police officers, medical examiners, forensic laboratory scientists, anthropologists, and entomologists, to mention just a few. And all this in addition to processing crime scenes! Fictional instruments give test results at warp speed, and crimes are solved in forty-two minutes. Because of the overwhelming popularity of these shows, juries now expect forensic evidence in every case.

The books in this series will take you to both old and new forensic sciences, perhaps tweaking your interest in a career. If so, take courses in chemistry, biology, math, English, public speaking, and drama. Get a summer job in a forensic laboratory, courthouse, law enforcement agency, or an archeological dig. Seek internships and summer jobs (even unpaid). Skills in microscopy, instrumentation, and logical thinking will help you. Curiosity is a definite plus. You must read and understand procedures; take good notes; calculate answers; and prepare solutions. Public speaking and/or drama courses will make you a better speaker and a better expert witness. The ability to write clear, understandable reports aimed at nonscientists is a must. Salaries vary across the country and from agency to agency. You will never get rich, but you will have a satisfying, interesting career.

So come with me into this wonderful world called forensic science. You will be intrigued and entertained. These books are awesome!

—Carla M. Noziglia MS, FAAFS

Prologue
From the Diary of Captain Javier Estefan Alonzo De Seville Officer of the Francisco de la Guerra Expedition into the far reaches of New Spain

(Translated from the Castilian dialect by Allen Roger Chesterton, Master's Degree Candidate, Northern Arizona University. The original manuscript is property of the Northern Mountain Museum, Flagstaff, Arizona)

Entry for September the fifth, the year of our Lord fifteen-hundred-and-forty

This has been a most unsettling day.

Around mid-day, the advance scouts spied a wide canyon, and at its throat enormous buildings. Shortly after, the entire troop came within view of the chasm. Our commander was eager to investigate more closely, as were we all. We proceeded to march at campaign speed, but the canyon and buildings tricked our sense of perspective, and we did not arrive at the entrance until twilight.

An awed hush fell over all of the men as we entered the canyon. Within the maw of the valley were clusters of buildings so large and finely constructed that their magnitude and masonry outmatch the palaces and cathedrals of our homeland, yet we saw no inhabitants, no evidence of human occupants for many years past.

Then, with no warning, a young woman appeared in the path directly ahead of our company. It was as if she materialized from thin air. Her whole body seemed to cast off a ghostly light, illumined unnaturally from head to toe. She was modestly clad in a finely woven garment that extended from neck to ankle. Her face was gaunt, but her eyes were unusually large. She appeared to be entirely unafraid of us, a marked contrast from the native women we have encountered hitherto on this expedition. One of the knights muttered, "Is this a ghost?" and the same thought was in all of our minds.

The girl spoke in a voice that echoed off the vast ruins beside us. "Turn back, O men from across the Great Water. There is no gold to sate your lusts here—but there is a power that inhabits these ruins, one ancient and dark. Your weapons will not help you, nor will your religion save you, if you venture further ahead. If you value your lives and your souls, go back as you came."

And then she was gone, as suddenly as she appeared. For only a moment, the expedition sat silent; even the horses were uncommonly muted. Then, Commander de la Guerra gave the signal for retreat. Our whole troop reversed direction and exited the haunted canyon more quickly than we entered.

So impressive was this girl's appearance that I have attempted to render her visage below.

(Translator's note: in the original manuscript, there is a crude line drawing inserted below the script at this point. Though simply drawn, the face is very distinctive. A digital image of the original manuscript, including this sketch, may be accessed via the Northern Mountain Museum Archives Web site).

Chapter 1
HUMAN REMAINS

Lupe Arellano held a broken fragment of jawbone between her thumb and forefinger. She touched it gently, making no more contact than necessary to avoid dropping the ancient piece of chin. The piece of skull evoked in her a sense of awe. This had been a person once, a unique individual like herself. For Lupe, that made it a relic of sorts, a holy object. The bone formed a tangible connection with some mysterious soul, now long departed.

"Amazing, huh?"

Lupe smiled and nodded at Mr. Chesterton. He was a large man, with curly red hair, a full beard, and a constantly cheerful countenance. Allen Chesterton had been Lupe's science teacher at Flagstaff Charter School during the previous school year, and he was one reason she had chosen to work as an intern at Northern Arizona University on this summer project. Lupe loved to watch *Bones* on TV and read mystery books about forensic reconstruction cases, so she had said yes without hesitation when Mr. Chesterton offered her the opportunity to assist him and the professor, examining a skeleton from the ancient past.

"Think this pile of old bones is worth missing that trip to LA?" Mr. Chesterton asked. The other members of Crime Scene Club were in California on a school-sponsored trip.

"Yes," Lupe replied. And she meant it.

"When I was a boy, I dreamed of finding ancient bones, secret documents." He grinned, remembering. "Now that I'm a slightly older boy, I get to come here, earn another degree, and do all that stuff I dreamed of."

"Can you imagine what someone might think handling *your* mandible, six hundred years from now?" added a woman who also sat with them at the table. Short in stature, round-faced, and cheerful, Professor Susie Tuwa was a Hopi archaeologist, renowned for her talent at "reading" skeletal remains.

"Have you been around human remains before?" Professor Tuwa asked Lupe.

"On our first Crime Scene Club case, we found a cave with the bones of men who robbed a train more than a century ago."

"I remember hearing about that. Didn't you find the Devil's Canyon treasure?"

"Just a few coins," Lupe replied. But those few coins had turned out to be quite valuable.

"That's a fascinating discovery," Professor Tuwa said. "What happened to the bones? Did an archaeologist study them?"

"Uh, no. They kinda got blown to pieces," Lupe said ruefully.

"Not the students' fault," Mr. Chesterton hastened to add. "There was a criminal who followed the CSC teens—he tried to bury them alive in the cave. The kids took a pounding—scared me half to death just hearing about it."

"Wow." The archaeologist seemed genuinely impressed. "Sounds like Crime Scene Club gives you some real adventures."

"It does that," Lupe agreed. "But tell me more about our case here." She pointed to the small pile of skull fragments that lay on the table between them.

"We're looking at fragments of a skull—plus a few other assorted bones—that park rangers found a decade ago at a site called Una Vida in Chaco Canyon National Historical Park, New Mexico," Professor Tuwa explained. "Are you familiar with Chaco Canyon?"

Lupe shook her head.

"It's an Anasazi site, isn't it?" Mr. Chesterton offered.

"Yes," the professor replied, "but archaeologists prefer to call them 'Pueblo Ancestors.' The word *Anasazi* comes from the Navajo tribe, and means 'ancient enemies.' But for those of us with Hopi or Zuni roots, they were our great-grandparents. And the Navajo also have traditions that they traded and intermarried with these people. So it's better to think of them as 'ancestors' than 'enemies.'"

"Was there a television special about Chaco Canyon?" Lupe asked. "Now that you mention it, I remember seeing parts of a show—there are some really big buildings there, right?"

"That's right," Tuwa replied. "Pueblo Bonito, largest of the so-called 'Great Houses,' has more than six hundred rooms. Una Vida, where these bones were found, is somewhat smaller. To build all the buildings in the canyon, the Chaco people had to transport two hundred thousand pieces of wood— and all the lumber had to be carried in by hand."

"It would be a difficult project using computers and modern machinery—incredible that people without the wheel or steel could do it," Mr. Chesterton said.

"Even more amazing," Professor Tuwa added, "these enormous architectural complexes serve as a sort of observatory, lining up perfectly with the sun and moon at the solstice and equinox. The ancient engineers who built Chaco had unsurpassed scientific skills for their time in history."

"What time in history do these come from?" Lupe asked, pointing at the bone fragments.

"We haven't done carbon dating, out of reverence for the dead. We don't use dating techniques that would damage the remains. But we can figure a date because of the location of these bones. They were found inside a building that collapsed from fire. Ash and burnt wood at the site date to 1250."

"So this person wasn't buried properly?"

"No. In fact, the way these remains were positioned in the room suggests this person was—it's hard to say this gently—discarded there, prior to the fire."

Lupe cocked an eyebrow. "Discarded? Sounds like a murder victim."

Susie Tuwa chuckled. "Don't get too excited— this isn't your Crime Scene Club. That's only a rough guess. We'll learn much more about this individual as we investigate the remains scientifically."

"So what do we do with these bones?" Lupe asked.

"First, we sort and assemble them. I'd say we have a fairly complete skull, as well as a complete right humerus and a complete right ulna. We'll examine the arm bones more closely, and we'll carefully piece the skull together."

"What else might we learn about him? Or her?"

"We may be able to figure out sex, age, diet, health, and cause of death. We'll also use computer imagery to reconstruct the person's facial image."

"So we'll be able to see what he or she looked like?"

"Pretty much."

"Awesome."

"What will become of these remains when we're finished studying them?" asked Chesterton. "I know the university works hard to honor Native remains."

"They'll be returned to the appropriate tribal group, in order to be properly buried," Professor Tuwa replied. "Part of our job is to connect this individual to his or her tribal descendants." She sighed. "For over a century, museums pillaged graves and thousands of Native bones sat piled in boxes on shelves. We have great respect for our ancestors, so this rude handling of their remains was a sacrilege for us. In part because of NAG-PRA, scientists now recognize that Native Americans are *people*, not specimens, and in many cases museums have returned our ancestors to tribal caretakers so they can be buried with appropriate ceremonies."

Lupe stared at the small pile of bones. "I feel like we should have a name for these . . . remains."

"Fine idea," the professor replied.

"How about 'Una Vida Man' or 'Una Vida Woman,' after the place of discovery?" Mr. Chesterton suggested.

"As soon as we know what gender this person was, that will be his or her name," Professor Tuwa agreed.

Mr. Chesterton and Professor Tuwa decided it was time for a coffee break, and Lupe ambled down the hall to get a soda from the machine. As she pulled a cold can of out of the dispenser, she thought, *I wonder if this could be Ken Benally's great-great-grandpa? Or one of the people his ancestors fought or traded with?*

Ken had been a senior at Flagstaff Charter the previous year and one of the most outstanding members of CSC. He was a policeman's son, and Lupe admired his obvious skills in detective work. He also had a Navajo heritage.

Unfortunately, her relationship with Ken had gone sour; in fact, it threatened to destroy the club's camaraderie. Ken had a steady girlfriend, Jessa, who was also a friend of Lupe's and member of the club—but throughout their first two cases, Lupe had sensed Ken's attraction to her, an attraction they both denied out of respect for Jessa. Then, while on their third case, Ken had kissed Lupe— just as Jessa walked in on them. *Officially*, Jessa and Ken were now broken up. *Officially*, the three of them were friends. *Officially*, there were no romantic feelings between Lupe and Ken. But in the privacy of her mind, she wondered if Ken didn't still feel something for her. And as for her feelings for him . . . She preferred not to dwell on the topic.

Still, she decided to send him a text message. Ken was working with his uncle on the family ranch, and she didn't want to call him and risk him breaking his neck when he tried to answer the phone while roping a bull—just the sort of thing Ken would do, she thought.

Lupe punched in the words:

```
Hey KB! I'm at NAU. Investigating
old bones from Una Vida NM. Your
g-pa?
```

The two adults were returning from their break, so she headed back into the room, where Professor Tuwa began to explain forensic reconstruction techniques. It was hours later, after she had left campus, that Lupe noticed a return message on her phone. Flipping it open, she read:

```
Lupe, I wouldn't touch those bones
if I were U. Very dangerous.
```

A New Name
The year 1247 (according to the Western way of keeping time)

She sat still, unflinching, as the sharpened bone, dipped in mineral dye, jabbed again and again into her cheek. It hurt. How many times would the older woman pierce her flesh, before the tattoo was complete? Against her wishes, a tear trickled from the corner of one eye. Yet she would not wince, she would not cry out. No. She was determined to be immovable as the towering rock of Sacred Mountain, brave as a she-bear. She must persevere

because, on this day, she was no longer a child. These lasting signs on her cheeks and chin, parallel lines marked with blue and red ink with dots in between, marked her as a grown woman, and her bravery under the needle was part of the transition to adulthood. Be strong. Don't move.

Just days before, she had been a girl, chasing her younger siblings through the rushes beside the River-That-Runs-Through-Red-Canyons. Their village of rounded earth huts lay at the top of a cliff above the river. Here, the People could see far around them, yet have access to the life-giving waters below.

The children were supposed to mind the nets stretched across the river, to pull out pike when they became enmeshed, and bring them fresh to camp for cooking. But she had known the fish, once caught, wouldn't go anywhere until they finished playing. So she had laughed and yelled, pursuing her little sisters and brother through the tall vegetation.

Then, just as she tagged her sister, the younger child pointed and exclaimed; "Ooh, blood!"

She twisted around, looked down at her white deerskin dress, where a dark spot was forming.

Her other sister laughed and clapped her hands. "Your change has come. You will be a woman now."

And so, four sunrises later, she sat in her aunt's earth lodge, with three older women murmuring and exclaiming around her, as she received the markings of womanhood. As they applied the tattoos, the women, in turn, spoke to her about the responsibilities of maturity.

"You are fair. Many young men will desire you," her mother explained. "Now you have an awesome ability—your womb holds the Creator's power to make a new person. So be very careful. Don't listen to men's promises. Those who desire you will flatter. They will speak sweet but false words. Wait . . . wait for a young man who possesses wisdom, strength, and bravery. Wait for the one who will join with you in the two-become-one ceremony, in front of all the people."

"Now you must think of others before yourself," her aunt joined in. "You aren't a child anymore. Life is not games and dolls. You are a woman of the People. You must concern yourself with our survival together, with finding wild food plants, with mending the fish nets so their prey cannot slip through, with skinning and butchering the game we depend on for life."

The third woman, her older cousin, who held the needle, added her counsel. "You must become wise now, and remember all that you hear. Remember what you've learned about the ways of Mother Earth and her children. Though men defend us in war and hunt for our nourishment, we women hold the sacred traditions—and our tribe's very survival depends on the knowledge we keep."

At each pronouncement, the girl blinked both her eyes to show she understood and would comply. She trembled, not from the pain of the needle, but from the weight of responsibility. *A woman, now. A woman of the People.*

Her cousin put down the needle. The three examined her face, critically. "Well done," her aunt affirmed. The others nodded.

"Up!" Her mother commanded.

She stood, though her legs were stiff from sitting.

"Out the door!"

She pushed aside the hide flap and stepped from the ceremonial earth lodge, blinking, into the glaring sunlight.

The People stood before her, waiting. In front of the assembly, Sage Woman, her wrinkled skin

wrapped in fine white rabbit-skin garments, leaned on her cane. "Know what to do?" Sage Woman asked.

She nodded. "Run—with all my might."

"How you run will reveal the course of your life," the elder affirmed. "Now—*go!*"

Though still light-headed from the pain of the facial tattoos and from a night of fasting, she took off like a bird racing over the desert floor. The others ran alongside her. As she ran, her feet seemed to take on a life of their own. Faster she went, and first the older people, then the middle-aged, then even the younger men fell away behind her. She felt like the wind, flowing easily up and down red sand hillocks, dodging bushes and small cacti in her path.

Finally, she came to the finish post, a stake in the ground, topped with a bison skull painted red with ochre. She stopped and leaned over, panting. A minute later, the young braves caught up with her, then the others. Finally, Sage Woman reached the group, limping at a brisk pace on her arthritic legs.

"Well done!" Her wrinkled face creased into a smile. "For thirty seasons, I have watched girls become women in this changing ceremony. None have run as you did today." Sage Woman turned to address the crowd. "Hear me, People of the Earth Lodges. Never again will any of you address this woman by her childhood name. She has a grown-woman name now. And her name is. . ." The young woman and the people gathered around her waited, in hushed silence. "Her name is Naqali— She Who Runs Ahead—a name of honor, because of the strength and speed she has shown us today."

The crowd murmured and repeated the young woman's new name.

Sage Woman turned back to face Naqali. The smile on her face vanished. "There is one more trial on the way to adulthood."

"I know."

Sage Woman pointed to a tiny earth lodge near the finish pole, with smoke pouring from a hole at its top. "You must remain in the place-between-worlds, until you see your future."

Naqali nodded her agreement and walked on shaky legs to the sweat lodge. She crawled through the narrow entrance, then knelt by a pile of stones heated by coals. She removed her jewelry, knowing the intense heat might scorch their shape onto her flesh. Then she poured water from a gourd over the stones. She felt her body grow hotter, breathed in the stifling vapors, as she repeated these actions again and again.

The tiny room began to spin around her, and her vision blurred. She saw only mists. Then, enshrouded in the stifling vapors, she saw a flame. The fiery image expanded, became a circle, then a spiral. At the tip of the fiery spiral was a sharp form, like a dagger.

Then, she heard screams, cries of pure terror. She trembled, genuinely afraid. She had never heard such agonized voices, and they seemed to be right next to her in the stifling confines of the lodge.

At last, the sounds died away, and she again saw the wooden beams and earth walls of the tiny enclosure. She opened the door cover and took deep, desperate breaths. Stooping, she returned to the bright light of the ordinary, outside world.

Sage Woman stood alone outside the sweat lodge, waiting for her. "The worlds parted?"

"They did."

"Tell me what you saw."

"A spiral."

"Which way did it turn?"

She gestured, indicating a sun-wise motion.

"Tell me more of its shape."

"It had a point like a dagger."

"What else did you see?"

"Not see, but hear." She recounted the horrifying sounds.

Sage Woman appeared troubled. For long minutes she pondered, then gave an interpretation of Naqali's vision: "The spiral you saw is a tribe and a power. They cut through other peoples like a knife through skin. They have their origin to the north, but they migrated to the land of endless sunshine in the south, and now they have come back—at least a part of them—to trouble the People." She paused, apparently frightened by her own pronouncement. "They bring great evil . . . sadness . . . pain. Those are the cries you heard."

Naqali shook. "Why did Creator show such awful things to me? I am nobody."

"No." Sage Woman shook her head. "You are somebody—somebody special. You are the strongest young woman of the People. When the evil reaches us—and it will come soon—the survival of our tribe will rest on your shoulders."

For the first time in the long ordeal of her womanhood ceremony, Naqali allowed tears to flow from her eyes. "I–I don't want all this."

"Of course you don't." Sage Woman placed a weathered hand on the young woman's shoulder. "No sane person would. But you are special, and you must defend the People. Even if doing so should lead to your doom."

Chapter 2
A MYSTERY

On day two of her summer project, Lupe found herself alone for most of the morning, except for the grim company of the Una Vida bones. Mr. Chesterton was translating ancient documents at the university library, and Professor Tuwa was doing tests in an adjoining lab.

So Lupe tried to make herself at home with her bony companion. She had printed out a picture by the Mexican artist Posada—a funny sketch he made for the Day of the Dead, showing two skeletons, dressed like a cowboy and a bargirl, dancing a jig—and she taped it on the wall beside a large illustration of the human skull that Professor Tuwa had provided. On the edge of the table she set her MP3 player and a small set of speakers, and she alternated between playing Tejano and rap, depending on her mood.

Growing tired of her recorded tunes, she turned off the player and hummed: "The chin bone's connected to the . . . other piece of chin bone. The other piece of chin bone's connected to the . . . other piece of chin bone." Her exciting summer project wasn't feeling so glamorous at the moment; it was more like the world's craziest 3-D jigsaw puzzle: all these little bitty pieces of bone had to fit together somehow to form a head.

Lupe stuck a fresh stick of plastic in the back of the glue gun and plugged in the tool. *Just like Mom uses for her craft projects.* Whenever she had a match, the teenager placed a tiny drop of the melted gooey substance on one bone, then pressed it against the other. The amazing thing was—it all went together. Piece by tiny piece it was starting to take the shape of a skull.

She had sent another message to Ken:

`What do u mean? What danger?`

She was still awaiting reply, so when her cell phone buzzed, she flipped it open quickly. But it wasn't from Ken. Instead, she read:

`Hey girl, wuzzup? Wish u were in LA. Surfer boys hot, hot, hot! And we have a real mystery. Dead body on shore. Investigating, will keep u posted. The undead rule! Maeve`

Maybe I should have gone to California, Lupe thought. She imagined the other girls from the club—hanging out with ripped blond beach-boys, investigating a real LA murder mystery—while she sat in this little room, piecing together fragments of skull.

She jumped when the door swung open suddenly and Professor Tuwa breezed into the room. "How's it going?" asked the archaeologist.

Lupe held up the results of her morning's work for inspection. The lower and upper jaws were mostly in place, along with a large part of the nasal bone and a bit of the cheek. "Not going to tell us much so far, is it?" Lupe asked.

Susie Tuwa smiled and picked up the partially reconstructed bones, staring at the fragment like Hamlet contemplating Yorick's skull. "I'd say that it is—a *she*."

"How can you tell?"

"Too soon to be sure, but notice the narrow chin on the mandible, and here where you've started on zygomatic bone it's rather rounded. Males have squarer chins and sharper cheeks, as a rule."

"So this is 'Una Vida Woman.'"

"Probably."

"I'm missing a tooth in the lower jaw."

"Like this one?" The professor pulled a molar out of her lab coat. "I borrowed it to look under the microscope this morning."

"Did she have a good dentist?"

"No, but the poor woman could have used one."

"Bad, huh?"

Professor Tuwa pulled a chair up to the table and produced a pencil, which she used as a pointer. "See the cavities in the back of this tooth here . . . and the side, here?"

"She should have brushed daily."

"Wouldn't have helped. I doubt she ate much sugar, but that wasn't her problem. See how thin the enamel is, from the middle to upper portion of the crown?"

"I'll take your word for it."

"It's a sign of malnutrition. At some point in her life, she almost starved to death."

"Oh." In an instant, Lupe's feelings toward her bone-puzzle changed. This wasn't just a project; it was a person of her own gender, who had struggled with malnourishment.

For most of the past year, Lupe had fought a running battle with anorexia. She had never admitted her problem until after she became involved with CSC. Now, she forced herself to eat, snacking through the day as best she could, since full meals were a challenge for her. It was tough to get food down, a struggle to look at herself in the mirror and not see fat (though everyone else said she was way too skinny).

"This is very strange," Susie Tuwa murmured, continuing to stare at the tooth.

"Weren't a lot of people starving in those ancient days?"

"They were," the professor explained, "but the hungry ones lived *outside* Chaco Canyon. There are indications that members of nomadic tribes— perhaps the ancestors of modern Navajo, Apache, and Ute nations—struggled for survival in that era. Meanwhile, the residents of Chaco tended to be overweight."

"So Una Vida Woman didn't belong where the park rangers found her?"

"Nope. Especially considering the angular surfaces on top of the crown." Susie Tuwa pointed her pencil at the upper part of the tooth she held.

"I don't understand. . ."

"Pueblo Ancestors were agriculturists, masters of dry-farming like the Hopi are today."

"And?"

"Most of their diet consisted of corn. They ground the kernels into fine meal for baking piki bread—like my grandmother still makes back on Third Mesa."

"And this relates to the tooth?"

"Pueblo Ancestors ground corn into flour using two rough stones, what archaeologists call mano and metate. As the two stones rubbed together, microscopic pieces of igneous rock would break off and become part of the corn meal. So Pueblo Ancestors invariably have terribly flat, ground-down surfaces on the *top* of the teeth from a lifetime of chomping on stone."

"Ah." Lupe understood now. "Una Vida Woman is turning out different from what you expected."

The professor nodded. "She belonged to one of the outlying tribes. So what was she doing at Una Vida?" As Susie Tuwa stared at the bones, her frown deepened.

"What're you thinking?" Lupe asked. "You look as if something's wrong."

"I can't quite define it, but . . . it seems like there's something *missing* from this skull."

"Missing? Did it get lost? Wouldn't that have happened easily over the years?"

The professor shook her head. "There's something not right about this woman's skull. I need to think about it some more."

Lupe felt a chill go down her spine. Maybe the CSC members in LA weren't the only ones to come across a mystery.

Chapter 3
WEYAKA

Despite Sage Woman's dire words, two changes of season passed without misfortune for Naqali. In fact, her fourteenth summer was the happiest of her life.

On the third full moon of the warm season, a runner came racing into the camp, calling out, "There are people headed this way—men, women, children, and dogs, carrying all their belongings."

Sage Woman pulled herself up from the reed mat on which she rested and squinted at the runner. "Did you see them closely? What manner of people are they—builders of the Great Houses? Invaders from the south? Or those who dwell in round-houses, like ourselves?"

"I spoke with them. They share our tongue— well, almost. Some of our words are different, but we can communicate."

"What brings them our way?"

"They come from the direction of the rising sun, and they say that the four-footed ones grow scarce there, and fish no longer inhabit the streams as they once did."

"So they move toward us to establish a new village where there is more food?"

The runner nodded.

"By what right do they claim to share our land?"

"Their head-man says he is third cousin to your brother. His name is Head-Like-Stone."

Sage Woman gave a surprised chuckle. She turned to Naqali, who stood nearby listening. "Tell your sisters to cook up deer and fish. We feast tonight with our far-away relatives."

Although the newcomers brought grim news, the two small tribes celebrated together that evening. The hunters swapped stories of their exploits and compared weapons, while the children laughed together, and the older women more quietly exchanged the histories of their tribes.

Naqali assumed the role of a host, walking between the fires, offering fresh pieces of well-cooked venison, sweet-berry mash in stone bowls, or herb tea served in baked-clay mugs. She stooped beside a handsome young man. He appeared to be a year or two older than she, lean but muscular. Intelligence flashed behind his eyes. "Would you like anything?" she asked.

"I would like to sit and chat with a lovely young woman."

"There are a number of pretty women among the people," she said, her eyes lowered.

"What are you called?"

"Naqali. It means Runs Ahead, from my womanhood ceremony. What is yours?"

"Weyaka."

"Tall Elk. How noble." She gave him a teasing smile.

"I did not choose the name—it was given me."

"On your becoming-man ceremony?"

"Yes."

"We have the same custom. Did you go alone into the wilderness, with only a knife—no food, no water, no sandals?"

"I did."

"And you fared well?"

"I returned dragging the meat and antlers of elk-brother."

"You killed him—with only your knife?"

The young man shrugged. "I was fortunate. He had separated from his herd, and gave himself to me. Creator must have sent him."

Naqali grew more interested. This hunter was as modest as he was skilled. "You . . . have wives?"

"I have no wife."

"But you're a fine hunter—surely you could support a family."

"Yes, if I found someone worth marrying. What about yourself? Is there a fortunate young man?"

"I do not have a husband."

"Aren't you getting a little old to be. . ."

"I'll marry when I wish." She tried to change the subject. "Tea?" She offered a mug.

Weyaka nodded, took a sip. "Made from the finger-plant. We had that where we came from, too. This is good for quenching hunger, and it helps broken bones to heal more quickly."

She looked at him, surprised. "You know herb-lore?"

"Some."

"Most men don't bother to learn it."

He shrugged again. "When times are hard it's good to learn all you can from life."

She glanced up at the stars, bright in the clear sky above the dancing sparks of the campfires. "Do you know the names of the star people?"

"That one we call the Bear, and that one the Hunter. It's good to know their places in the sky. Then we can tell which season approaches—and sometimes learn of our destinies."

"What do you see for your future, Weyaka?" she asked.

He placed his hand over hers. She sucked in her breath and tensed, but she did not pull away. "I see an intelligent, beautiful woman—someone I hope to know much better soon."

In the coming days, Naqali took counsel with her parents and elders. They in turn spent many watches of the night talking with Weyaka's relations, and then reported back. "He's a fine young man—the union would be good for both our bands."

And so, just as the nights grew colder and aspen leaves changed from green to yellow, Weyaka danced around Naqali's lodge, as the people came out to exclaim, "Come out! Come see! There's going to be a two-become-one ceremony today."

The couple stood side-by-side before all their people. Sage Woman placed a buffalo robe over

their shoulders, proclaiming, "May you share the same blanket—may your bodies always warm one another."

After that, Head-Like-Stone offered them a two-mouthed clay canteen and pronounced, "May you share together water and fire, berry and meat. May you be one now, in hungry-times and in abundance. Drink, both of you, from this one vessel—and so become one."

As soon as the couple finished drinking together, the two tribes began to chant and clap. Naqali and Weyaka shuffle-stepped around the earth lodges, and all the people, men, women, and children, followed them, matching step for step. It was the happiest day of Naqali's life.

The star people migrated in their courses, and the season of orange leaves gave way to winter. Snow blanketed the high desert country. There were no berries to pick now, and the streams froze over. It was the time of year to live off game; but this winter, the elk and deer were scarcely seen.

Sage Woman grew so thin that her skin seemed to hang off her bones, and she rarely moved from her place near the fire. The littlest sister of Naqali caught a coughing illness and died. The elders were so weak and hungry they could barely perform the four-day ritual of Journey-to-Spirit-World songs, and even the hunters who bore the child's body away from the camp were so famished that they struggled to pull the wood-fork stretcher.

After the ceremony, the men sat around a fire in Head-Like-Stone's lodge; Naqali and the other women sat quietly in the shadows.

"Darkness spreads, from our former lands to yours," Head-Like-Stone said sadly.

An elder of the people nodded assent. "It comes from the Great Houses. They take more and more. They become fat while the tribes around them waste away."

"They're greedy—like animals. So let's attack them—take them down like the senseless creatures they are," suggested a thin but wiry warrior.

Head-Like-Stone shook his head. "They may act like beasts. But we are still human. It is wrong to attack those who have not attacked us. Besides, for as long as we can recall, the Great House people have been friends—even shared in marriage—with the Earth Lodge People."

"You're afraid," the younger man accused. "You've heard the same rumors we all have—there is a great evil that's taken over the Great House village. Witchcraft runs them. You're scared to attack."

"Will *you* lead the war band against the Great House people?" Head-Like-Stone asked quietly.

The young man dropped his gaze and stared into the fire, ashamed.

"We don't need to attack them." All eyes turned toward Weyaka. "We only need to enter their territory—take from the herds remaining there, just as they have taken game from our lands."

"Yes," another hunter agreed. "I have heard a bison herd winters between Great House Village and our own lodges. Let's send our hunters—*all* our hunters—in case we encounter their men. One good hunt, just a quick in-and-out of their lands, and we'll have enough meat to feed the People through the rest of this winter."

Head-Like-Stone looked thoughtful. "It's not a bad plan. Only . . . with all the hunters gone, who will defend the People?"

"Who would attack us except for the Great House tribe? And they'll be following our men," the hunter replied.

"I . . . I'm not sure." Naqali could see the struggle on the chief's brow.

Naqali squared her shoulders. "We'll be all right. The women of the People can guard ourselves while you men are away." A gasp shot through the circle. A woman had dared to speak at a hunters' council! Naqali stood just beyond the illumination of the fire, well aware of the taboo she had violated, and equally aware that her unexpected words had fallen with great weight upon the assembly.

A full moon later, Naqali wished more than anything she had not spoken out of place. The men were still gone; only the women, the feeble elders, and the children remained huddled by diminishing fires, chewing at the last remnants of dried meat, dreading the freezing chill that gnawed at their bones. Two more children had died of the coughing disease, and no one had strength for the burial rites.

Then, one night, Sage Woman left; she simply walked out of her lodge into a howling snowstorm. No one followed; they knew she had chosen to journey to the spirit world. She would not take any more food from the mouths of the People, not in the starving time.

As their energy waned, the people spoke little. Even children and infants became still; they moved as if they were sleepwalking. The women did not speak, but they cast searing glances at Naqali, who had spoken out of place and encouraged this fate.

Isolated even from her own mother and siblings, Naqali crouched beside a dying fire. Where were Weyaka and the other hunters? Why didn't they return?

She knew something awful must have befallen them.

Chapter 4
BAD MEDICINE

Professor Tuwa's comment about something missing fired Lupe's curiosity. At the end of the afternoon she asked the older woman if she could stay in the lab and work longer.

"I can't give out my keys, so you'll be locked out of the room after you leave for supper."

"That's all right. I don't need supper."

"Sure? You don't have much fat on you."

"I'm okay. Really. I'll get snacks from the machine down the hall."

The archaeologist nodded. "I've never seen a summer intern who wanted to spend more time with the bones than the assigned hours. Suit yourself."

"Thanks, Doctor Tuwa!"

Hours later, Lupe was still hard at work on the puzzle of Una Vida Woman's skull. She was so focused that she hardly noticed the time go by until she looked out the window and saw it was dark. She turned off her media player and listened. The whole building was silent: no footsteps or voices. Only then, did it occur to her: *It's kinda creepy working alone at night with a pile of ancient bones.*

Lupe was reaching for her MP3 player, seeking the comfort of music, when she thought she heard a bumping noise in the corner of the room.

"Who's there?"

Nothing. She was still alone.

Could there be a mouse in the room? She walked over to the shadowy corner, but she found no evidence of any life besides herself in the chamber. And yet she felt the tiny hairs on the backs of her arms lift. She turned back toward the table, then froze.

A cold draft tickled across the nape of her neck, so sudden and tangible it felt like an icy fingertip brushing against her skin. Lupe shuddered, glanced at the air vents. They were turned off—so where would a cold draft come from?

All right, she told herself, *this is what comes from watching too many* Ghost Hunter *shows. Pull yourself together, girl.*

She strode back to the table and pressed the button on her player, then turned up the dial on the little speaker set, filling the room with the boom-thump of hip-hop. *More like it.* She picked up the half-finished skull, looked into the nearly complete eye-sockets, and said, "We'll have you done in no time."

Wham! The crash made her jump, clutching her chest. Breathing fast and shallow, she spun around to see that two boxes, filled with pottery and other artifacts, had fallen from a high shelf onto the floor. Their contents now lay scattered across the room. There was absolutely no reason that she could see for why they would have fallen.

Without any further thought, she flung open the door and bolted down the hall, then out the door, into the comforting night air. She put a hand against a column to steady herself, took long deep breaths, tried to focus. What on earth happened in there? What was going on?

Lupe pulled out her cell phone. She didn't really want to call Ken Benally because . . . well . . . he might get the wrong idea, might think she was pursuing him, might imagine she was hoping to be more than friends.

On the other hand, she told herself, she needed more information. She punched in a speed dial number she had forgotten to remove and waited a moment. "Hey Ken, it's Lupe."

"Oh, ah, Lupe . . . whazzup?"

"Yeah, uh, nice to uh, talk to you, Ken, I mean. . ." *Get a grip, chica.* "Listen, something weird happened here tonight."

"Where's here and what's weird?"

"NAU, I was working with those bones, and . . ."

"Uh-oh."

"What?"

"I told you—those bones are bad medicine."

"I know. I thought maybe you were joking, but . . ."

"But what?"

"Never mind. Just tell me why you said they're dangerous."

"They're from Una Vida, in Chaco Canyon, right?"

"Yeah."

"That place is big-time haunted."

An hour before, she would have scoffed at this. Instead, Lupe glanced up toward a second-story window, the only light left on in the building, the one she had forgotten to turn off when she ran out the door.

"Haunted? Why? How?"

"I don't know much about it. Stanley Peshlaki could tell you a lot more, though. He knows the old traditions like the back of his hand."

Lupe knew and respected Mr. Peshlaki; he was the painter and medicine man who CSC had worked with on their first case. She still had his cell number in her phone. "Think he'd mind if I called and asked him about that?"

"He wouldn't mind."

"Thanks, Ken. Uh, I guess that's all I needed from this call."

"You sure? You sound a bit . . . rattled, maybe?"

"No. I'm fine."

"Sure?"

"Yeah."

"Okay. Well, if you're like, bored anytime, you can always come out here to the ranch. It's really nice. We can ride horses out in the desert, or walk with the sheep, or—"

"Yeah, right, I mean, *no*—not right!" What was Ken trying to do, get them in trouble again? "Gotta go." She snapped the phone shut.

First the falling boxes, now this silly talk with Ken. Was she losing her mind?

There's something comforting about morning. After a sleepless night, Lupe pulled her red scooter up in front of the lab a few minutes before nine, just as Professor Tuwa arrived.

"Doctor Tuwa, before you go into the lab—"

"Hi, Lupe, you're here bright and early."

"Yeah, listen, I gotta explain—"

The professor turned to look at her. "What are you so worked up about?"

Lupe recounted the experiences of the previous night. "So there's this mess on the floor," she finished.

"Relax," the archaeologist assured her, "it's not like I'm going to fire you—you're a volunteer, after all."

Lupe missed the joke. "But . . . what . . . what made it fall?"

"I should have warned you, those are flimsy old shelves. I've seen them collapse in other rooms. I keep asking the university to pay for new ones, but they're so cheap about things."

"So it wasn't a . . ." She bit back the word "ghost." It sounded so silly in the morning light.

The professor looked at Lupe with her brows raised, waiting for her to finish. When she didn't,

Professor Tuwa turned briskly. "Come on, sounds like we've got a little cleanup to do before we start the day. I told you, you need to eat a healthy supper. If you try and get by on sodas all day, it just stresses you out."

Later in the morning, Lupe had finished piecing together the front of the skull when Professor Tuwa came in holding the two arm bones, which she had taken to an adjoining room for microscopic examination. Mr. Chesterton had spent the morning beside Lupe, translating his old Spanish manuscript. He said he "just felt like having company," but the teenager suspected he had heard about her fright the night before and wanted to make sure she didn't feel spooked again.

"Anything interesting?" he asked the professor.

She set the ulna and humerus bones on the table. "Yes." She pulled a magnifying glass from a large pocket on her lab coat. "Look at those little markings."

Mr. Chesterton and Lupe took turns examining the bones.

"What are those?" Lupe pointed to lines on the bones.

"I've seen cuts like that on bones in a criminal case," her science teacher replied. "It was a case of. . ." He hesitated, looked at Lupe.

"Hey, Mr. C, it's me—Lupe. I took a bullet in the chest on our first case, remember? I crawled through a cave with spiders. You don't have to sugarcoat stuff."

Mr. Chesterton sighed. "It was a case involving cannibalism," he finished. "This psycho left knife marks like this on his victims' bones."

"Except these were made by a stone blade—there are microscopic traces of black obsidian in one of the grooves," the archaeologist put in. "However," she went on, "these could *not* be marks of cannibalism."

"Oh, good." Lupe was sincerely relieved, despite her bravado. "Hope you don't mind me asking, but—how do you know that?"

"These were found in Chaco Canyon, at a time when the site was inhabited by Pueblo Ancestors."

"They didn't have any Hannibal Lecters?"

"They did not. *Nothing* could be more repugnant to Hopi or Zuni people than cannibalism," Professor Tuwa explained. "We have tremendous respect for the dead, and I'm sure the same was true for our ancestors. Some things change in a culture, but other things stay constant—and our abhorrence for desecration of human remains is the kind of tradition that would remain unchanged over a long time." She paused a moment, then asked, "Do you know where the word 'cannibal' comes from?"

The other two shook their heads.

"When Christopher Columbus arrived at the new world, he thought he was in the Orient, so he called the Natives 'Canibes'—that is, subjects of the Khan. Of course, he was foolishly mistaken about that—along with a lot of other things. He claimed these indigenous people ate their fellows, and he used that as an excuse for their enslavement and slaughter."

"That's awful!"

"It is, and in our scientific work today we need to carefully avoid jumping to false conclusions. After all, even the dead should be innocent until proven guilty."

"May I ask," Mr. Chesterton inquired politely, "how you account for those markings?" He pointed back toward the two arm bones.

"A few similar cases have shown up at other sites. Some archaeologists think the ancient Chaco people practiced ritual cleaning of bones, as preparation for a secondary burial."

"That sure sounds less sinister." Though it was still a little creepy, Lupe thought.

"Yes—and it would fit with the general cultural pattern of honoring the dead."

Lupe wanted to believe her. After all, Professor Tuwa was an *expert*, known worldwide for her ability to draw accurate conclusions based on ancient forensic evidence. But then Lupe remembered the sudden, unexplained cold draft on her neck the previous night, the crashing boxes, and Ken's words about Una Vida being "big-time haunted." Suddenly, cannibalism didn't seem so far-fetched after all.

Chapter 5
DESPERATE JOURNEY

Naqali slept poorly, troubled as she was by cold, hunger, and worry. When she did sleep, she saw the pained face of Weyaka, crying out, "Help me—free me!"

She sat up in bed, rubbed her eyes, saw that the only stick in the fire pit had burnt to ashes. Sage Woman's words came unbidden into her mind: "You are special, and you must defend the People." She drew the bison robe tighter around her and shivered.

Crawling on her hands and knees across the floor, she peeped out the door flap; no one else was stirring. She took a chert knife from the dirt floor, where it lay beside the last few meager scraps of dried meat. The blade was dull. Using an antler tine, she carefully chipped at the knife's edge until it was sharp. Then she tucked it in her belt and shrugged her thickest fur cape over her shoulders. A pair of fox-fur lined boots reached up to her knees. Across her chest, she placed the strap of a gourd canteen filled with water.

Finally, she took a sacred pouch her mother had given her, a finely beaded talisman that contained a rainbow-colored shell from the Great Water, a symbol of beauty, and a turquoise bear fetish for strength. She kissed the little pouch and slipped it over her neck. Naqali would need all the good fortune she could get on the journey that lay ahead.

In the doorway, she hesitated. *What kind of fool am I? The hunters have met some terrible fate, and I will track them? The People are starving—and won't I just die alone in the wilds?* She almost turned around, but again she recalled Sage Woman's words: "The survival of our tribe will rest on your shoulders."

Naqali whispered aloud to no one, "If I don't go after them, who will?" She slipped out of camp into the pale light of a winter dawn.

All that long day she headed east, guessing her direction from the sun and from the shadows it cast behind her in the evening hours. That night, she found a shallow cave in the side of a small, cone-shaped red rock hill, where she curled up and slept fitfully.

The next day, she had little strength, but she pressed on. Was the air actually getting warmer, or was her mind playing tricks due to starvation? She plodded wearily, forcing one foot to follow another, her feet numb, her belly gnawing. Grasping her talisman, she breathed a prayer for strength.

And then, ahead of her, she saw a doe. It was as gaunt as she was, stumbling over the low bushes as it walked on shaky legs. "Sister Deer," Naqali whispered, "it is your life or mine." She stepped toward it, her legs faltering, and the four-footed one tottered away from her. In a slow-motion dance the two walked on, panting and aching, the woman and the animal, each struggling ahead for life itself. After what seemed an eternity of painful pursuit, the deer stumbled in a rabbit hole. Naqali fell exhausted across the doe's back and slit its throat with her sharpened knife. "Thank you, friend. Your sacrifice will be remembered," she mumbled into the animal's ear as they both tumbled onto the cold earth.

That night she filled her empty stomach with the fallen deer's meat and slept beside its carcass. Next day, strengthened by that meal, she walked more quickly. As she headed toward the rising sun, the land sloped lower and the air grew warmer. She found a cactus still in fruit and ate the pulpy food greedily.

Just before nightfall, she came across a small creek. She fell on her hands and lapped water like a dog before filling her empty gourd flask. *Creator is good*, she thought. *It's not my fate to die of thirst or starvation.*

On the fourth day of her eastward trek, Naqali spied condors circling lazily on their great wings, eyeing some crumpled object a stone's throw to her left. Drawing closer, she heard moans.

A human! When she knelt alongside the body, he was so disfigured she didn't recognize him at first. Then she realized he was the young hunter who had encouraged attack. His skin was cracked, his lips lacerated by dryness. A hand's length of wooden shaft protruded through his side, topped with the longest obsidian spearhead she had ever seen.

Naqali forced open the man's cracked lips with her trembling fingers and poured water down his throat.

His eyes opened, blinked. "Naqali?" he croaked.

"Save your breath," she told him. "You're near to the spirit world."

"I'm good as dead," he rasped back. "The others . . . all captive."

"What happened?"

He took a deep, rattling breath and winced. "Four days out, we came upon . . . a woman." He paused, gathering strength. "Beautiful . . . different . . . not like us." He shut his eyes, rested. Naqali feared he would die before finishing his account, but one eye re-opened and he resumed. "She said . . . come with her. She would give . . . food for the People. Your husband, he says no. But we didn't listen. Our doom."

The dying hunter's eye rolled, and for a minute she thought his spirit had departed. Then he spoke again. "We went with her . . . then, there were warriors . . . tall, with strange weapons. They attacked. Took all but me."

She cradled his head, tried to speak comfort. "You did your part. Rest now."

His eyes flashed. "Where will you go?"

"To rescue Weyaka and the others."

"No!" His cold fingers grasped her elbow. "Turn back. There's only death ahead." A moment later, he let go of her arm and slipped into the spirit world.

Sinister Surgery

During lunch break, Lupe tried to call Mr. Stanley Peshlaki. She only got a recording: "Hello there. I'm out with the sheep or doing a ceremony. If I decide it's important I'll call you back, so leave a message if you want to."

"Mr. Peshlaki, this is Lupe Arellano from Crime Scene Club. I need to talk to you—please call me soon."

By mid-afternoon, Lupe had the skull almost entirely put together.

"Nice work," Professor Tuwa told her.

"But you were right: something is missing. The top of her head's not here."

Mr. Chesterton and the archaeologist both leaned forward to see. At the top of the skull was a neat two-inch circle. "Those pieces have been missing about eight centuries," Professor Tuwa said. "Very neatly cut out."

"Cut?" Lupe frowned, feeling a little sick.

"Yep. Peri-mortem incision."

"I'm sorry?"

"This piece of skull was surgically removed right around the time of death."

Lupe put a hand on the table top to steady herself. "Wow. You can tell that because. . ."

"The nature and symmetry of the cuts. There's nothing jagged here." The professor ran a finger around the inside of the hole. "So it was done with a very sharp instrument—obsidian, no doubt. The cuts are smooth, which means they were made while the bone was still soft. If the cutting were done very long after the time of death, we'd see more little chips on the perimeter of the incision, due to hardening bones."

"Okay. And what does all this mean?"

"I've seen cuts like this before, down in Mexico," Mr. Chesterton answered, "on the skulls of Aztec sacrificial victims. The sun priest ate their brains

after death, hoping to absorb the cunning of fallen adversaries."

"Allen, you're being dramatic again." The professor frowned at him. "First cannibalism, now eating brains. You're working on a master's degree—not writing the script for a *Temple of Doom* sequel."

Mr. Chesterton looked offended. "I wasn't trying to be funny. I saw them in the National Museum in Mexico City. The label said that—"

"Museums just want to make money—and they do that by being sensational," the archaeologist retorted. "Once again, what people commonly write about the Aztecs—or rather, the *Mexicas* if we want to be scholarly—is based on the accounts of European invaders, who wrote lies to justify slaughtering an entire civilized empire."

"The Conquistadors were brutal," Mr. Chesterton agreed.

"Hey, you're talking about my ancestors now," Lupe cut in.

"You mean the Aztecs or the Conquistadors?"

"Yes." Lupe grinned. "Both."

"Archaeologists don't necessarily agree with the Spaniards' accounts of ancient Mexican sacrifices," Professor Tuwa resumed. "The incisions in skulls that you label 'brain-eating' are more likely evidence of surgical procedures, done in order to remove excess liquid from patients' brains."

"They did surgeries?" Lupe was amazed.

The professor nodded. "Your ancestors were really smart people."

"They did surgery with stone knives?"

"Actually, obsidian is as sharp as any surgical steel produced by science. A freshly chipped obsidian blade is only a molecule wide at the cutting edge. If they put me under the knife, I might ask the surgeon to use Stone Age technology."

Lupe touched one finger to the skull. "So she died from an operation?"

"Could be."

"How old was she when that happened? Can you tell?"

Professor Tuwa pulled out her magnifier and peered for a minute at the dome of the skull and at the jaws. "Based on the lack of fusion of the cranial sutures, the fusion of the epiphyses on the humerus, but not on the ulna, and from the wear and tear on teeth and jaw, I'd say she was a teenager. Maybe a bit younger than you are."

Lupe winced. "Why would someone try and save her life by surgery, and then just discard her body by throwing it in a room?"

"Spoken like a true detective." Mr. Chesterton gave her a smile.

"Good questions, I have to admit," the archaeologist agreed. "We may find the answers—and we may not. But for now, I think it's time to call it a day."

As the adults headed for the door, Lupe's cell phone rang. She stayed behind to talk to Stanley Peshlaki and explain why she wanted to talk to him.

"Can you make it out here tomorrow afternoon?" he asked.

"After I'm done here at NAU. But—I don't have a car."

"I'll talk to your friend, Ken Benally. He's working on a ranch right next to mine. He'll give you a ride."

"Oh, I, uh. . ."

"Unless you have another ride."

"No." She shrugged. "Okay. Well, if Ken doesn't mind driving all the way into town, that is."

Peshlaki laughed. "Of course he won't mind. See you tomorrow then."

"Thanks." Her hands felt clammy as she pictured herself stepping into Ken's truck. Last time the two of them had been together near Peshlaki's place in the Canyon. . . .

Enough. No more thinking about that.

After she closed the phone, she sat down at the table, put her chin in her hands and contemplated the ancient head. Now that she was alone in the room, except for Una Vida Woman, she found herself once more unsettled by the weathered skull staring back at her with its top missing, like a Jack-O-Lantern with the stem cut out for a candle. She wanted to believe Professor Tuwa's theory, and she really did admire the professor's expertise—but despite the archaeologist's assurances, the skull's incisions, combined with the cuts on the arm bones, would point a modern detective to murder done by the sickest sort of psychopath. This eight-hundred-year-old cold case was growing more bizarre—and more sinister. Lupe couldn't help but think, *Something really awful happened to this poor girl.*

Chapter 6
THE PRIESTESS

Naqali covered the hunter's body with a simple cairn built from rocks, and then she continued her journey toward the east. That night, she slept beside a spring under the cover of tall, thorny bushes.

At mid-sun the following day, Naqali saw the smoke of lodge fires. Heading toward the ascending plumes, she came upon an outlying settlement of the Great House People.

She had heard of—but never seen—their homes. While this was only a small outpost, it nonetheless amazed her. Noticing an unfinished wall, she examined its construction: an uncountable number of little square stones piled atop one another, the cracks between them filled with straw, then daubed with clay and earth to form a tall, smooth wall. The outpost was entirely constructed in this manner; she thought it must hold a couple dozen rooms, some piled atop one another two and even three stories tall.

The small settlement was beautiful—and intimidating. Its inhabitants wore clothes made of finely woven plant materials, as smooth as finely tanned leather but lighter and decorated with beautiful squared patterns. The women plaited their hairs in large spirals on each side of the head; the men wore their hair long beneath thin woven caps that covered their necks. Off to the side of the village was an enclosure made of earth banks, and within it young men kicked a round ball made of a strange substance that allowed it to fly as if by magic from whatever it touched. She had to admit that their dwellings, dress, tools, and weapons were all superior to those of her own tribe.

Naqali did not wish talk to anyone; if these villagers knew her purpose in coming, they would take her captive—or do worse. Yet she desperately needed food, and her water was running low.

"You—Earth-Lodge woman!" She was surprised to hear herself addressed in a badly accented form of her own speech. She turned to see an elderly man, a trader, who sat beside a wooden frame filled with pottery, fabrics, and tanned skins.

"You speak my language?" she asked, surprised.

"Travels Far speak many tongues," the old man replied with a grin. "Knows how talk Earth-Lodge People, Great House People, Buffalo Hunters, and Salmon Fishers even." He gave her a gap-tooth smile. "What your name, pretty one?"

"Naqali."

"Means 'She Who Runs Ahead.' Fine honor name that is. Want to buy something from Travels Far?"

"Food. I need food."

"Don't have with, but these folks be plenty fat, and you look lean-in-the-ribs. If something you have to pay, I make deal. Get you corn on the cob, freshly killed venison, frog legs maybe even." He smacked his lips. "Got something to pay?"

Naqali hesitated a moment, then reached into her sacred pouch and pulled out the rainbow-color shell. She needed food or she would have no strength for the rescue; the special shell would do her no good if she died in the attempt.

"Ah." Travels Far seemed genuinely impressed. "Nice thing for trade." He took the shell, hopped up, and hobbled quickly into the outpost. Before long he returned, balancing three bowls filled with simmering meat and vegetables. Naqali had not felt such pleasure since last she shared Weyaka's embrace. She gobbled ravenously, not stopping until every bowl was licked clean.

"Earth-Lodge people must be hungry," the gnarled trader mused. "Hungry were the hunters led to Great House tied up."

Naqali's gaze snapped to his face; then she glanced quickly away, afraid she had revealed too much.

"Don't fear," Travels Far said quietly. "Live off their wares yes, but I no friend of Great House People."

"What happened to my husband and the others?" Her voice shook as she asked the question.

"The Priestess took them."

"Who is this priestess?"

"From the Endless Sun Land she came, couple of winters ago. Priestess she was there, of the Mexica tribe. Big person of the Mexica was she—but not most big. Warriors with her, as many as four sets

of hands. Tall, dressed in panthers' skins. Sharp, deadly cutting sticks with black stone blades they carry, and spear-throwers what cut through shield and bone."

"So . . . this priestess—did she conquer the Great House people? For many generations my people traded with the Great House tribe and we lived together in peace. Now they've changed. Is that because she took over the Great Houses?"

"Took over—that she did. But not by warring. No, they welcome her. Priestess is beautiful, like the sun in its strength, like rain on dried earth. Men—at least stupid ones, which most of them be —follow her, like moths to torch."

"What's her name?"

"Quetzalxochitl."

Naqali frowned at the unfamiliar word. "What?"

"Ketz-al-zoe-she, priestess of the Sun God."

"So, they made her their leader?"

He nodded and made a face. "Fools."

"And it's her doing that the Great House Tribe has broken its treaties and spoiled the earth of fish and game?"

He nodded. "Greedy she—like hunger never filled, more and more food and wealth she piles into the Great Houses. Good for their tribe, yes. As for others, you grow thinner. Maybe soon dead and gone."

"What makes a person act that way? Is she without sense, like the beasts?"

"Oh, no. She is cunning, with great wisdom. In Mexica tribe, she had power—but not enough.

Two brothers of hers princes, they try kill her. But she escape, Panther Warriors with her. Often those who are mistreated, mistreat others in turn." Travels Far glanced both ways, leaned closer to Naqali and whispered. "More power she seeks always. Her lust unstoppable."

Despite the warmth of the mid-day sun on her head, Naqali shivered. "Has she taken other people as captives, beside our hunters?"

"Oh, yes. Many."

"Where does she keep them?"

"In the first of the Great Houses in canyon. House of Rain they used to call it, but now, House of Make Thin Then Die."

Naqali felt faint. "She starves and kills her captives, then?"

The trader kept his face close and his voice low. "Starves them so cannot resist. Then sacrifice."

"Sacrifice?"

"High Tower at Tall House, she made into temple for Sun God. There, she takes victims. Panther warriors drag up steps. With big knife, she cuts out heart."

Naqali felt her knees buckle, and she slumped to the ground. She sat in an undignified heap, trying to catch her breath. "I don't believe it."

"True is, and worse."

"Worse? What could be worse? Even animals don't do such things."

Travels Far bent low and whispered in the young woman's ear. "They say, after sacrifice, she takes skin from bone of victims, grinds their flesh to make corpse powder."

"C–corpse powder?"

"Great witchcraft power it gives. Shape-shifter she, becomes wolf or bear or black wind."

Naqali grasped her mouth, trying not to retch. After a couple of deep breaths, she said, "You're crazy. No human being could do that."

"Used to think like you I. So did all the people. Now, Great House Village becomes evil. These things she does, and worse."

Naqali looked at him, afraid to ask, unwilling to hear more. He whispered, "Eats the brains, after killing strong, smart ones. Strong magic it gives her, to make curses."

"Why don't the Great House People rise against her? Have they become mad?"

"Some fight, but Panther Warriors are terrible and strong, and makes she witch darkness against the rebels. Resist Quetzalxochitl? None can."

"But the Great House People are many. She can't control *all* of them by force."

"No." He shook his head sadly. "But fat she keeps them—fed well and wealthy, while other tribes makes she hungry. The Great House people are changed now, twisted by greed, evil."

Naqali pulled herself to her feet. She had heard enough.

"Where you go now, woman of the People?"

"To the Great House, to free my husband."

"Oh, no. Too late. Maybe he dead by now."

"Then I go to *kill* this so-called priestess, to avenge Weyaka."

"Oh no, little one. No, no. Turn back." He held

out her rainbow-shell. "Take back trade. Gift from me, food is. Take lovely shell, for trade with people on way back to your village you go."

She shook her head. "Keep it. This trade has been a bargain. You gave me information—much more valuable than food."

"No." He bobbed his head up and down. "Insist. You take back." He pressed the shell into her hand.

She, slipped it back into her pouch. "You're a good man, Travels Far. I'll always remember you in my prayers."

"Prayers save for yourself, unfortunate young woman. Madness for you to go there. You face something more dark than mere flesh and blood."

Chapter 7
TORMENTED SPIRIT

The skull spun slowly on a metal coaster as a thin red laser beam moved up and down, reflecting back onto mirrors surrounding the bone. Lupe and Mr. Chesterton watched in quiet wonder while Professor Tuwa concentrated on her laptop computer monitor. As the laser beam traced Una Vida Woman's bones, a three-dimensional image appeared on the computer.

Lupe could not recall later how long it had taken: Half an hour? An hour? More? But the process came to its end when Professor Tuwa flipped a little switch by the mirrored box and declared, "That's an excellent scan."

"Amazing!" Lupe stared at a detailed image of the skull as it spun slowly around on the monitor's flat screen. Save for the color, it was the perfect likeness of the ivory-colored, time-weathered relic that it replicated.

"Without destroying anything, or risking damage to the remains, now we can create an image of her face," Professor Tuwa explained. "First, we'll add muscle."

"How does the program know what depth of muscle to put on?" Mr. Chesterton asked.

"This program is based on hundreds of CAT scans from real people. It combines them to create an average depth and shape of musculature over the image of the skull." She entered data, and a few minutes later, the image of the skull was wrapped in a layer of virtual flesh. "That's a good average musculature," the professor explained, "but we know that shortly before death, she was malnourished. So I'm adjusting . . . cutting back a small percentage of muscle depth on her cheeks." The picture became slightly narrower. "And," Professor Tuwa went on, "we can factor in her age as well." She selected the age range 12-15 from a drop-down menu and the image altered slightly again.

The other two stared, transfixed by the way that this jigsaw puzzle of broken bones was transforming into a young woman, right before their eyes.

"Let's put some skin on these muscles." The professor scrolled through a list of skin shades, selected "Native American, Southwest, " and moments later the image on the screen was clearly a face, though still without eyes and other features.

The morning went by as Doctor Tuwa added lips, which she explained were a bit thin, since malnourishment robs the body of collagen. Then eyebrows appeared and finally a pair of large, dark eyes. "She has unusually wide sockets," the archaeologist explained.

Mr. Chesterton stared at the face on the monitor. "She was a striking girl,"

Lupe giggled. "Especially since she didn't have any hair."

Professor Tuwa scratched her chin. "This is where it gets real iffy. The question is—what kind of hair do we give her?"

"Not blond and curly," Lupe said.

"Though she does look a bit like Shakira," Mr. Chesterton countered.

"Shakira has naturally straight hair," Lupe snapped back. "She permed it to look like a gringa."

Professor Tuwa suggested, "How about long black hair with a center part?"

After this change, they were all silent for a moment, looking at the face on the screen. A determined, intelligent, and fine-featured young woman stared back at them.

"Call me crazy but—I swear I've seen that face before," Allen Chesterton exclaimed.

"Been doing some time traveling lately?" Lupe joked.

"Very funny. No, really, she looks familiar, but I can't place her."

"I would say," Professor Tuwa said, "that this reconstruction confirms our earlier guesses. She doesn't look like my Hopi relatives or Zuni Pueblo friends. Her features are Athapascan—which nowadays would make her Navajo or Apache. Since the Chaco area is ancestral land to the Navajos, I'm thinking the Navajo Nation should claim her as one of their ancestors."

"I'm going to visit Stanley Peshlaki this afternoon," Lupe said. "He's a Navajo *haatali*—a medicine man. If you can print out her face, I'll show him the picture and see what he thinks."

"Great idea," Professor Tuwa agreed. "I'm always thankful for a second opinion."

Mr. Chesterton shook his head. "Who does she remind me of? I just wish I could place her."

As they exited the building that afternoon, Ken pulled up in his pickup truck.

"Hey, Benally, good to see you," Mr. Chesterton greeted him. "How's it feel to be graduated?"

"Not much different," Ken told him. "I've been so busy it hasn't sunk in yet."

"Working?"

"On my uncle's ranch this side of the Rez. I like cowboy work, and it gives me and Dad a nice break from each other."

He does look like a *ranchero*, thought Lupe, noting Ken's dust-covered Stetson. She walked to the passenger side door.

"Oh, I see you two are back—" Mr. Chesterton began.

"No!" shouted Lupe.

"I'm just the taxi driver, we're just friends," Ken hastened to explain.

"He's a handsome one, isn't he?" Professor Tuwa whispered, standing behind Mr. Chesterton.

Lupe reddened and pretended she hadn't heard the remark.

"Got plans for college?" Mr. Chesterton asked the young man.

"Coming here to NAU in the fall," Ken explained.

"What major?"

"Criminology. They have an excellent department for that."

"That's great!" the science teacher exclaimed. "Maybe you can come over some afternoons and help us out at Crime Scene Club?"

"I'd love to," Ken replied.

"We'd better hurry," Lupe said, pulling herself into the cab. "There aren't any lights on the way to Peshlaki's place."

"You sound like a city girl," Ken chided her.

"I *am* a city girl. Grew up in the *barrio*, remember?"

Ken put the truck into drive and waved at the two adults as he headed out of the lot.

Lupe squirmed in her seat as they drove north on I-89. She was as afraid to connect with Ken emotionally as she feared connecting with him again physically. The time he had held her felt so good, so right, and so . . . awful. Especially the look on Jessa's face when she found them kissing. After that, Ken told Lupe he didn't like her—in front of the whole club, no less. Whether or not that was true, she wasn't about to forgive him for it. They drove on in awkward silence.

As the sky darkened, they bumped along a dirt road and finally stopped in the valley that belonged to Stanley Peshlaki. His home was a traditional eight-sided log and earth Hogan. Lupe noticed he still had a tin chimney sticking out through the top, while beside the ancient-style home stood an array of solar panels. A flock of thick-coated Churro sheep grazed near the building. Beside the Hogan was a rough wooden corral, holding half a dozen horses.

Lupe started for the door, but Ken grabbed hold of her elbow. She jumped at his touch, as if lightning had hit her—but the electric sensation wasn't entirely unpleasant. He let go immediately. "Wait," he whispered. "It's not polite to barge in on elders. He'll come out in a moment."

After a few minutes, Mr. Peshlaki came through the door, dressed in worn jeans and a flannel shirt, wore tooled cowboy boots, and a new-looking iPod, hanging on his belt.

"Come in, come in," he said as he shook both teens' hands.

"I love the new paintings," Lupe commented as they seated themselves on a comfortable couch. She pointed to a couple of pastel-covered canvasses hanging from the wooden beams. "They look more abstract than the ones you usually do."

"I get bored doing the same things," he explained. "And I'm sick of the way people stereotype Native art. So I'm mixing it up a bit."

"I like it," Ken agreed.

"Have a soda?" Peshlaki opened the fridge and gestured to a six-pack of Coke.

"Thanks," they both said.

"Now, you have some questions?"

Lupe explained her summer project and handed the haatali a printed image of Una Vida Woman. "We're wondering if she was an ancestral Navajo?"

He pondered the face for several long minutes. "She's Diné alright. She should rest in our ground. But . . . her bones were found in Chaco?"

"At Una Vida."

His brow furrowed.

Lupe continued, "She had strange cuts on her bones—and the top of her skull was cut out."

The man's eyes widened. "That's bad—but I'm not surprised, coming from such a cursed place."

"Why is it cursed?"

"We don't call it 'Una Vida.' For centuries before white people came, that place had another name. It was called *Asdzáá Halgóni Bikin*."

"What does that mean?"

"House of the woman who makes you thin by starving you," Ken translated.

Lupe felt goose bumps on her skin. "Why did they call it that?"

"A beautiful woman lived in the Great House there," Stanley Peshlaki explained. "She was a powerful witch, who lured young men into her dwelling, then held them captive, starved them—and killed them."

Lupe shivered. "The cuts and . . . missing portion on the woman's remains, would that be. . . ?"

Ken answered. "Witches make corpse powder, use it to—"

"Stop!" the elder commanded. "Some things we don't speak of."

"Sorry," Ken mumbled.

But Lupe had to know one more thing. "I— I'm going to sound crazy, but . . . something strange happened when I was alone working on the skull."

"You felt her *chindi*," the older man said matter-of-factly.

"Her. . . ?"

"Ghost," Ken translated.

Lupe looked from Ken's face to Mr. Peshlaki's, wondering if they were serious.

"She is a victim of witchcraft, a tormented spirit." The medicine man shook his head. "Every day you handle these remains, you place yourself in grave danger."

Chapter 8
HEART OF EVIL

Night had spread its black wings over the land by the time Naqali neared the Canyon of the Great Houses. She approached along the very edge of a tall sandstone cliff, doing her best to blend in with the shadows and shrubs. There was a guard house, consisting of four rooms, at the mouth of the Canyon. In front of it, a creek ran into the gorge.

Though the night was growing chilly, she cast off her garments, save for her deerskin wrap and medicine pouch. Her boots and cape she hid under a bush. Then, silently, she slid into the stream. Ever so carefully, she pulled herself along the rocky floor of the river, allowing only her mouth to come up and quietly suck in air. Slowly, slowly she moved along the river bottom, past the guard house. Then, when she was safely downstream, she slid out of the freezing water and huddled behind a rocky crag, catching breath and warmth.

Ahead, she could make out lights in the windows of an immense structure—much larger than any man-made object that she had ever beheld. *The Great House—where that priestess holds Weyaka and the others.*

Again, she blended into the shadows and crevices of the cliff edge, drawing near the enormous building—or rather, a complex of buildings, as she now saw. She approached to within a stone's throw, then hesitated, studying the fortress-like dwelling that reared into the night sky before her. Its sides were six or seven times her height, and windows were all set into the wall well above her reach. There was a single opening at the front of the building. The door was guarded. *Those must be the Panther Warriors.* A half-dozen men were positioned like statues, the skins of great cats draped over their shoulders, mouths and fangs of the beasts atop their heads. Each carried a shield covered with the feathers of exotic birds and long, narrow wooden sticks with sharp obsidian edges. *No way to get past them.*

She looked again at the walls. They were covered with smooth earth, as the outlying settlement had been, offering no handholds for climbing. Naqali quietly worked her way around the back of the complex. *Ah, there!* She spied a ledge, protruding from the cliff side, its summit just an arm-span away from a window on the back wall.

Carefully, moving by touch rather than sight, she climbed the rocky escarpment. The rough stone chafed her arms and legs. She felt for handholds, slid her fingers until she touched an indentation or knob to grasp, pressed her aching body into the rock's surface, and wrapped her toes around slight outcroppings to push upward.

A crescent moon was in mid-sky by the time Naqali pulled herself onto the summit of the rock formation. Barely breathing, she peered into the window near her. Light came out of it, but she heard no voices, saw no movement, only the flicker of a fire, hidden from her sight. Reaching the window would be a stretch—but she thought she could make it.

"A woman of the People," she whispered to herself. She grasped the pouch hanging on its strap around her neck. Then, summoning all her strength, she leaped.

The earth-covered wall and its window flew toward her in the dark.

Closer.

Closer.

No! She was falling too fast.

She reached up and stretched her fingers as high as she could reach. Her fingers clung to the bottom of the window as her chest slammed into the wall. Desperately, she pulled upward. The wall leaned slightly inward, so by pressing every part of herself onto it she could gain slight traction.

Finally, she dragged herself through the opening, falling onto a smooth floor. She was in a warm, spacious room, with thick woven blankets on the walls, painted pots and weaving implements on the floor. In the corner, a fire crackled in a rounded stove. Thankfully, she was alone in the room. She pressed her ear to the wall, heard no one, so she slipped out into an adjacent passageway.

For what seemed hours after that, Naqali navigated a maze of tiny rooms, mostly unlit and unoccupied, and the dark tunnels between them. In some directions, she heard voices. She thought—but was not sure—that she heard two tongues spoken; one she guessed to be that of the Great House People, the other that of the strange tribe from the South.

Like a mouse, she stealthily moved through the dark recesses of the labyrinth. Once, she almost walked into a pair of Panther Warriors, but she melted back into shadow just in time to watch them stride past, their rippling chests and strange shields so close she could have touched them.

At last, descending inward and downward through the great structure, she heard the sound she had longed to hear: men's voices, speaking the words of the People. She carefully peeked around the edge of an oddly shaped door.

Weyaka! He and the other hunters were sprawled on the floor, their hands and feet knotted tightly by woven fiber cords. Their ribs showed through their chests. And just inside the door, stood a large Panther Warrior, half-again as tall as Naqali.

In the warrior's left hand he held a fighting stick, its sides edged with sharp black stone. In his right hand was a curved stick, a spear-thrower, and a wicked-looking spear like the one that had killed the hunter who died in the desert.

Naqali quickly pulled her head back and leaned against the wall in the dark, pondering. The only thing she could think of to do went against everything in her better nature—and yet she had no choice. She felt on the floor, found a stone. It was as long as her hand, round and smooth. She said a quick prayer, took a breath, and began the rescue.

First, she put her mouth beside the door and made cooing noises, like a woman in love. At the same time, she extended her bare leg and waved it back and forth. Then she pulled herself back into the shadows.

She only had to wait a moment. The guard stepped through the door, stood in the darkened outer room, trying to see in the dark. *Stupid animal.* She brought the stone down on the guard's head with all her might. He groaned and lay still on the floor.

She leaped into the captives' room. "Naqali!" Weyaka cried. "Am I dreaming?"

"Shh. No sound! We're not out of here yet." With the fallen warrior's fighting stick, she quickly sliced through the ropes binding the hunters. Stiff and starving, they staggered to their feet and hobbled as quickly as they could out of the room.

Warily, she led them back through the maze. Again, it seemed a long nightmare. This time she was encumbered by the others; in their weak condition, the men could not move as quietly as she could. More than once, she feared a cough or footstep would give them away.

After several failed attempts to find their way out, they came to a large door leading to a small courtyard. At the other side of the courtyard was the entrance she had seen from outside, with the guards standing stiffly in front of it.

"What now?" she whispered.

"You still have the guard's weapon?" Weyaka asked.

She nodded.

"Let me wield it. Their backs are to us. They suspect nothing. We outnumber them . . . we can prevail."

Naqali lifted the cord from around her neck and slipped her sacred pouch over her husband's head. "It's brought me good luck—it will guard you, too."

They kissed; then Weyaka turned to the hunters behind him. "Are you with me?"

They murmured assent.

"All right. One, two . . . now!"

The men ran as fast as their thin legs would carry them. The first of the Panther Warriors Weyaka brought down with a single swing of the fighting stick. Another hunter grabbed the fallen man's weapon, and then things moved too fast for Naqali to follow. In what seemed the blink of an eye, the guards were down.

But not before one of them let out a scream in his strange language. Yells sounded from elsewhere in the huge building, and torchlight reflected off the walls of the Great House.

"Hurry! Go!" Naqali cried.

The next instant, hands like iron gripped her waist. She screamed, kicked. A Panther Warrior held her fast, jabbering in a language she could not understand.

The men of the People were already outside the wall, escaping into the dark. Weyaka lingered inside

the gate waiting for her. He saw the man grab her, yelled her name, and ran toward her.

P-f-f-t! A spear flashed through the dark and sliced into Weyaka's leg. He fell onto one knee, then stood again painfully. At the same instant, another Panther Warrior grabbed Naqali's legs, tackling her. The two enormous men held her down, like a deer in a trap. She saw more of the warriors running across the courtyard toward her stricken husband.

"Weyaka!" she screamed. "Go. You can't help me now. The People need you."

He stood crouched, his face twisted with anguish. Then another of the hunters dashed back through the doorway, grabbed Weyaka by the arm. "Run!" He pulled Weyaka behind him.

"I'll come back for you," Weyaka shouted. She watched as he hobbled away, vanishing into the dark. Then, rough hands pulled her to a standing position. She was surrounded by dozens of angry warriors.

Face from the Past

The ride back from Peshlaki's place was a bit more relaxed than the way there. Lupe and Ken talked about Navajo curses, ghost stories, and television shows. It was like old times, when Ken was just a friend, a real friend.

Then, as he pulled into her drive, he put a hand on her shoulder. She looked at it but said nothing. "I really miss you," he said. "Seriously, if you ever want to hang out, go see a movie. . ."

Something inside her snapped. She jumped out of the door, slammed it shut, then stuck her face through the open passenger side window. "You're a jerk, Ken, you know that?"

"Huh?"

"Heard anything from Jessa lately?"

"No, I . . ."

"How about Veronika with a "k"—or have you forgotten her already?"

"Lupe—"

"You know you could've had Jessa back. She still loves you, but you broke her heart."

His mouth opened and shut like a goldfish gasping for air in a poorly oxygenated tank.

"But thanks for the ride." She turned and strode into her house, banging the door shut behind her.

The next day was Friday—the weekday Lupe didn't have to work at the university. She was just as glad, after the previous night's frightening story. She slept in late, had coffee for breakfast, and was watching a telenovela when the phone rang. It was Mr. Chesterton.

"I know it's your day off, and hope I'm not bothering you," he explained, "but I just now realized where I've seen Una Vida Woman before. Of course, it's just an odd coincidence, but—there's something you should look at. I thought if you're interested we could meet at the Campus Coffee Shop. Of course, it could wait. . ."

"I'll be right there."

She brushed her teeth, pulled her hair into a pony tail, got on her Vespa, and zipped along the road to NAU.

At the coffee shop, Mr. Chesterton said, "This is really weird. I realize, of course, that it's just a freaky random thing, but—"

"Out with it."

"All right, look at Una Vida Woman on this print-out."

"Yes? Same as yesterday."

"Now check out this." He slid a large photograph of an old document in front of her. The first thing she noticed was Spanish handwriting; then she saw the sketch.

"*It's her.*"

"Uncanny resemblance, I know."

"What *is* this?" She pointed to the photographed document.

"It's the diary of a conquistador in the sixteenth century who ventured into the ruins of Chaco Canyon. I've been translating it as part of my thesis."

"Whoa. Hold on." She looked at the date on the document. "Una Vida Woman died three hundred years before that."

He nodded. "Like I said, freaky coincidence, but I found it interesting."

"Mind if I read the diary?"

"Be my guest."

Some of the words were unfamiliar, but she could easily understand most of the finely handwritten entry. When finished, she said, "Too creepy."

"Yes, it's bizarre."

"I *knew* she was a ghost."

Mr. Chesterton shook his head. "I shouldn't have shown you this. You've been on edge this whole project. You need to eat healthier, cut back on caffeine, get more sleep—"

"Mr. C!" she interrupted, so loud that college students in the coffee shop spun around to look. Embarrassed, Lupe lowered her voice. "Just listen, it all fits together. The marks on the bones—she was the victim of something awful, like the witch Mr. Peshlaki told me about. So now she's a ghost, and that Spaniard saw her and I felt her in the room that night—"

Mr. Chesterton cut her off. "Lupe, I'm sorry. I didn't realize you were so worked up or I never would have showed you this. You're badly stressed. Think of everything you've gone through in the past months, that injury from the first CSC case, Maeve's accident, that thing with Ken and Jessa. . ."

"Don't patronize me." She practically spat the words. "Everyone has issues. But I'm telling you, this is a puzzle and now—the pieces fit."

"*If* you believe in ghosts."

"Well, how do you explain it all?"

"Everything has a rational explanation."

"So let's hear it."

"Professor Tuwa told us that there may be perfectly innocent reasons for the markings on the skull and the bones. The girl may have died in surgery, and the bone markings could be signs of respect."

"Go on."

"There are cold drafts in the building at night, and Doctor Tuwa said those were old, weak shelves that collapsed under the boxes."

"But what about this picture? That's *her*—three hundred years after she died."

"No, these are two portrayals that happen to look alike. Forensic reconstruction is guesswork, and sometimes even attempts to render modern faces from skulls can be way off. For that matter, maybe this conquistador was a lousy artist—this drawing could be quite different from the woman that he actually saw. There's no way to know if Una Vida Woman looked anything like the girl those Spaniards met."

"But they're so alike."

"Maybe she had descendants—this girl in the sketch could be Una Vida Woman's great-grand-daughter. Sometimes family resemblances skip generations."

"Stanley Peshlaki told me there was a witch who lived at Una Vida. She captured and killed people. He said the spirits of witch victims are—"

"Listen to yourself. Lupe, you're sounding like the narrator of a horror movie. I respect Mr. Peshlaki and his traditions—but every culture has stories about ghosts and witches. That doesn't mean they're true."

"So you don't believe in the supernatural?"

He shook his head. "I believe in things that can be weighed, tested, replicated. By limiting beliefs to what can be proven, humanity has developed electricity, modern medicine, computers."

"You know, you gave this same speech at the start of earth science class last year."

"Sorry, but you get my point. What about you, Lupe? Do you really believe in things you can't see or prove?"

"I've been thinking a lot, since this internship began." She paused, selecting her words. "I found a quote on the Internet, by a guy with your last name—G.K. Chesterton. I guess he's a famous writer. He said, 'There is a choking cataract of human testimony in favor of the supernatural.' And I've grown up hearing stories about the Virgin and the saints and miracles my whole life. I believe in science and sound reasoning, but I also know there's something powerful and important that I experience in my religion—and that's a good reason to believe there's a supernatural aspect to life." She paused, then resumed. "Believing in the unseen can be comforting, but also troubling in cases like this one. So I have to admit, it's kind of a double-edged sword. "

"Hey." Allen Chesterton looked uncomfortable. "I'm not slamming your beliefs, Lupe. You're one of my best students and I respect you. As a teacher, it's my job to challenge you, to make students think. So I'm just trying to help you clarify your thoughts. Do you really think a supernatural explanation is the best way to make sense of what you've experienced this past week?"

"I don't know, Mr. C. I just don't know."

As she drove home on her scooter, Lupe's head swirled with questions. She passed Scorsese's Pizza Parlor and waved at her friend Juana, who happened to be exiting the restaurant. At the same instant, an SUV squealed out of a side street. Lupe turned her head just in time to see an enormous chromed grill flying her direction.

Wham! Lupe rolled into a ditch, bruised and shocked. The big car had just missed her.

"Oh my God!" Juana cried. "Lupe, are you alright?"

Lupe looked at her torn jeans and the scraped skin on her elbow. She carefully rotated her limbs. "Don't think I broke any bones—but I'm gonna be wicked sore."

"Good thing you were wearing a helmet."

Lupe pulled off the plastic shell and examined where the front had scraped along the road. "Guess so." Then she spied her scooter, smashed against the curb. "Oh no!" She walked over and gently pulled it upright. One entire side was bashed in and scraped.

"Oh, your beautiful Vespa," Juana moaned.

Lupe sat down on the curb next to her scooter and put her head in her hands. Then she remembered Stanley Peshlaki's warning: "Every day you handle these remains, you place yourself in grave danger."

Chapter 9
THE VICTIM

The Jaguar Warriors stood over Naqali, eyeing their new captive. Then, their attention shifted to something behind her. Naqali turned.

Quetzalxochitl walked serenely across the courtyard, directly toward Naqali. Atop the priestess's head was a magnificent headdress of shimmering green, vivid blue, and bright yellow feathers. With each step she took, the feather crest waved. A closely formed garment of glittering green stones cupped the woman's breasts, and a large ring of glittering gold pierced her navel. From the waist down, she wore a skirt of raven feathers.

As Quetzalxochitl drew nearer, Naqali couldn't help but be transfixed by the woman's features. Her face was rounded, with full lips, a tiny chin, and gracefully curved nose. Her septum was also pierced by a golden ornament. There was something both splendid and unsettling about the Priestess's face.

As she drew within an arms' reach, Naqali realized what it was. *Her age*; the woman's eyes and bearing were those of an elder, yet her skin was taught and smooth like that of an adolescent. Naqali realized, with a chill, that the priestess was indeed a woman of years who somehow, by some unholy means, retained her beauty in its fullness.

The priestess reached out and took hold of the young woman's chin. She turned her captive's face one way then another, like a merchant would examine an animal for sale in the market. Her lips turned up at the corners, as one smiles when about to consume a particularly delectable berry.

"How kind of you to visit us—though it is a bit on the late side."

For the second time in a day, Naqali was astonished to hear her own language.

The priestess guessed her thoughts. "Surprised? Don't be. There isn't much I don't know."

One of the Panther Warriors stepped forward and spoke rapidly in the Mexica dialect; Quetzalxochitl poured out a rapid stream of lilting words in return. Then the priestess turned back to her captive. "He asked if we should track and kill your men. I told him, 'Let the little birds fly. I have the prettiest hen of the flock.'"

Naqali shut her eyes to clear her mind. As she did so, she once again heard the words of Sage Woman, as if the old crone were speaking across time: "You are special, and you must defend the People . . . even if doing so should lead to. . ." Naqali sucked in a deep breath and straightened her shoulders. *And I have defended the People, she thought. The hunters are freed. They will find food, and return home. Without them, the women, elders, and children would*

have died—but now the People will survive. I have fulfilled my destiny.

Quetzalxochitl brushed a long fingernail over the young woman's cheek, bringing her suddenly back to the moment at hand. "You *are* special," the priestess whispered, "and such a lovely surprise in this dreary season." She rolled her delicate tongue around the edges of her lips.

Naqali spat on the priestess. "You act so fine, but inside—you're nothing but buffalo dung."

The priestess's eyes became glassy, her cheeks taut. "The Sun God will take your heart." She made a motion with her fist, as if she were pulling the young woman's guts out. "After that, I shall feast upon your wisdom parts and grind your flesh into powder. So . . . off to the High Altar."

The priestess made a quick, slight movement with her hand. Two of the warriors gripped Naqali by the arms and dragged her away.

I have fulfilled my destiny.

Return to Mother Earth

"Don't worry. *M'ija*, I'll make your scooter good as new. I'm just glad my little girl is okay."

On Saturday, Lupe worked with her father in his garage paint shop, patching, buffing, and priming the damaged side of the Vespa. Normally, she would complain about the whine of machinery and smell of chemical compounds, but this weekend she actually appreciated them. It was nice to get her mind away from the bones, to do something that felt so ordinary.

In the afternoon, however, a text message interrupted her ordinary day:

```
Done examining remains. Will bury
on Monday. Peshlaki to do rites.
Hope you can come. S. Tuwa.
```

She sent back confirmation that she would attend and then made another call. The *haatali* actually answered his cell this time. "Mr. Peshlaki," she said, "I heard you're doing the funeral for Una Vida Woman. I just wondered . . . I'll understand if you say no, but . . . could I say a few words during the ceremony? I feel kinda connected to her."

"That would be fine," he replied. "You've taken an interest in her. In fact, you may be her best friend among the living. I'll give a nod when it's your turn to speak."

Lupe then phoned her priest, Father Ignacio. After she hung up, she wrote a few words on a scrap of paper.

Monday morning Lupe sat in the back seat of Mr. Chesterton's van, next to Professor Tuwa. Mr. C. drove, and a wooden box, draped with a finely woven Navajo blanket, sat on the passenger's seat beside him.

"The burial site is a couple miles down canyon from Mr. Peshlaki's home," Professor Tuwa explained. "When we arrive, he'll sing chants to put her spirit to rest."

Lupe pulled the reconstructed visage of Una Vida Woman from her bag. She glanced from it to the box, and shook her head.

"What's going on in that active little mind of yours?" Professor Tuwa wanted to know.

"It's frustrating."

"What is?"

"We've worked so hard on these bones, and we were able to bring her face back from the past. But there's so much more we *don't* know. Did she die from an operation or a murder? Was she hungry because of a drought or because someone starved her? Did she sing or dance? Who did she love? I wonder about her—and it almost makes me crazy."

"I understand," Susie Tuwa said softly. "When you handle someone's bones, there's a connection formed between the living and dead. Then you have to accept that we can only learn so much, and for every answer there are two more questions."

Lupe sighed and looked out the window at the red rock ridges and sandstone buttes of the high desert. So many people—Native, Latino, Anglo— had lived and died in this country, and only the land remained unchanged. Its inhabitants passed like a mist.

When they arrived, they found the haatili sitting beside a neatly dug hole in the ground. Lupe at first thought his clothes were faded, but then she realized his garments were covered with fine white ash.

About thirty feet ahead of the burial site, the ground fell away sharply, leading down into a deep gorge with a view of a winding river. It was a beautiful place for a grave, Lupe thought. "This was the site of a very ancient Diné village," Peshlaki explained. "I thought she might feel at home here."

Mr. Chesterton gently set the blanket-covered box in the ground; then the four sat around the grave and the haatali began his song, the plaintive tones of his voice rising and falling, his right hand lightly tapping his leg in a steady cadence. At intervals, he paused in his chanting to sprinkle corn pollen on the site.

Lupe was tired and stiff when Mr. Peshlaki finally stopped singing. He pointed to her and nodded. She stood, pulled a piece of paper from her blouse pocket and read aloud: "*La luz en las tinieblas resplandece, y las tinieblas no prevalecieron contra ella.* The light shines in the darkness, and the darkness does not overcome it. *Amén.*" She put the paper back in her pocket and spoke toward the ground. "We don't even know your real name, but we want to say that we're sorry if you had a bad life. Seeing the image of your face, you look like a special person, and I wish we could have been friends somehow. We've tried to take real good care of your remains, and we all hope you can be at peace." She sat back down.

Stanley Peshlaki handed shovels to Mr. Chesterton and Professor Tuwa, and they scooped dirt back into the hole. Then he pointed to a small pile of rocks, and Lupe joined the others in constructing a cairn. As they did so, the medicine man took

the two shovels they had used to dig the grave and flung them over the cliff edge, down into the river below.

When the rock shrine was finished, all four stood a few minutes in respectful silence. Then the haatali instructed them, "Brush away your footprints so the dead cannot follow, and take a few wrong turns on your drive back—for the same reason."

"We will," Mr. Chesterton promised. "Do you need a ride home?"

Mr. Peshlaki shook his head. "I feel like walking."

Just as they were about to step into the van, Lupe spied something glittering on the ground. She leaned down and picked up a piece of shell. "This looks like abalone, but it's so far from the ocean." She rotated it in her fingers; one side had turned the same hue as the earth, the other shimmered with the colors of a rainbow. "It must be really ancient—see how it's weathered?"

Stanley Peshlaki looked at it; then he folded Lupe's fingers over the object, indicating she should keep it. "A gift from the distant past," he said softly. "Must be we've made someone happy."

FORENSIC NOTES

CRIME SCENE CLUB, CASE #6

PROLOGUE

Evidence List

Vocab Words

potential
taxing
maw
magnitude
masonry
materialized
gaunt
sate
visage
apparition

Deciphering the Evidence

Commander de la Guerra will not let the
men leave their armor behind to lighten
their loads; he wants them to be prepared
for any *potential*—or possible—conflict.

Traveling at campaign speed is *taxing* for
the men; they find it difficult and tiring to
keep up such a pace.

The men are quiet as they enter the canyon
and peer down into the *maw* of the valley.
Maw means the mouth, throat, or stomach
of a hungry animal or greedy person, but
can refer to anything that seems like a gi-
ant hole ready to devour things or people.

In all their travels through this part of New Spain, the men have not seen structures with the *magnitude* and *masonry* of the buildings in the valley before them. Magnitude means size and masonry is typically construction made from brick, cement blocks, or stone.

What Does "Campaign Speed" Mean?

A campaign is a military operation, so to march at campaign speed would be to proceed quickly as soldiers would when carrying out a strategic maneuver.

The company of men is startled when a young woman suddenly appears in the path ahead of them. She seems to have *materialized* out of thin air.

The young woman's face is pale, thin, and bony; her *gaunt* appearance makes her look eerily ghost-like.

Who Were the Moors?

The Moors were inhabitants of northern Africa of Arab and Berber descent who traveled north and conquered Spain in the eighth century.

The girl instructs the men to turn back, saying there is no gold to *sate* their lusts there. Sate means to fully satisfy, as in an appetite.

101

The narrator wants to capture the girl's striking *visage* on paper, so he sketches her face in his diary.

Around their fires that night, the men don't speak of the ghostly figure they saw, but the narrator is sure the *apparition* is on their minds.

P.1 A map of New Spain in 1779, created for Santini's Atlas Universal by Jean Baptiste Bourguignon d'Anville (1697-1782).

Where Was New Spain?

New Spain refers to the territory in North America and the Caribbean claimed by Spain beginning with the conquest of the Aztec Empire in the 1520s through Mexican independence in 1821. It included the modern nation of Mexico, Central America north of what is now Panama, Florida, and a large portion of what was to become the western United States, including California, Arizona, Nevada, Utah, Colorado, New Mexico, and Texas.

What Was Plate and Mail Armor?

Plate armor consists of large metal plates worn for protection over the chest and sometimes the whole body. Mail armor is a flexible, mesh-like armor made of metal links or scales. It can be worn as a complete outfit or as separate pieces covering the head, arms, or legs. Mail armor is still in use today in gloves worn by butchers and in anti-shark suits worn by divers.

CHAPTER 1

Evidence List

Vocab Words

evoked
tangible
countenance
mandible
pillaged
sacrilege
camaraderie
persevere
transition
sacred
traditions

Deciphering the Evidence

The piece of human skull in Lupe's hand *evoked* in her a sense of awe. It brought out a feeling of wonder at the fact that this had once been a person just like her.

The bone formed a *tangible* connection with some mysterious soul from the past. Lupe is amazed that it was possible to touch such a holy object with her own hands.

Mr. Chesterton has a constantly cheerful *countenance*; his face always displays an expression of good humor.

Professor Tuwa asks Lupe if she can imagine what someone might think handling her *mandible* six hundred years from now. Mandible refers to the lower jawbone.

When Are the Solstices and the Equinoxes?

The two solstices occur approximately on June 22 and December 22. Solstice literally means "sun stands still," and refers to the fact that for half the year, the sun appears to rise further north each day, then it seems to pause, or stand still for a few days, and then the rising point begins to move south. This phenomenon is due to the tilt of the earth's axis in relation to the sun, which changes daily as the earth rotates around the sun. In the northern hemisphere, the summer solstice is the longest day of the year, and the winter solstice is the shortest.

The two equinoxes occur approximately on March 21 and September 23. Equinox literally means "equal night." The equinoxes are the two times during the year when day and night are the same length. On these dates, the tilt of the earth is such that the sun is exactly above the equator. In the northern hemisphere, spring begins on the vernal equinox in March, and fall begins on the autumnal equinox in September.

Professor Tuwa explains to Lupe that graves of Native Americans were *pillaged* for over a century by museums. Pillage means to take something from someone or someplace wrongfully.

The rude handling of Native American remains was a *sacrilege*; it showed disrespect for something considered sacred.

The members of Crime Scene Club share a spirit of easy-going friendship with one another, but Lupe's relationship with Ken, who was Jessa's boyfriend, has threatened to destroy the club's *camaraderie*.

As the older woman pierces her flesh to make a tattoo, the girl does her best to *persevere* through the pain. She knows that the ability to keep going even when it is difficult to do so shows her strength and bravery.

Having a tattoo applied to her face is part of the girl's *transition* to adulthood. She is experiencing the passage from one stage to another—from being a girl to being a woman.

The girl's older cousin explains that it is the women who keep the *sacred traditions*—the customs passed down through the generations that are to be respected and honored.

How Is Carbon Dating Done?

Carbon dating uses a radioactive form of carbon to determine the age of past things that were once alive. Anything on earth that lives contains the element carbon. In its most common form, carbon has an atomic weight of 12. C12 is a stable, or nonradioactive isotope, meaning it remains the same. Carbon also exists on earth in tiny amounts of the radioactive isotope carbon 14. Radioactive isotopes do not stay the same forever, but decay, or break down into other atoms over time.

C14 can be used for dating because of its radioactive half-life, which is about 5,700 years. A half-life is the amount of time it takes for half of the C14 atoms to decay into a different atom.

All living things have the same ratio of C14 to C12. After plants, animals, and people die, the C14 in their remains breaks down, while the amount of C12 stays the same. Therefore, scientists can measure the ratio of C14 to C12 in a skeleton and figure out, relatively accurately, how long ago that person died. However, because of C14's half-life, it is only useful for dating items up to about 60,000 years old.

The World of Forensics

Our English word "forensic" comes from the Latin word *forensis*, which means "forum"—the public area where in the days of ancient Rome a person charged with a crime presented his case. Both the person accused of the crime and the accuser would give speeches presenting their sides of the story. The person with the best forensic skills usually won the case.

In the modern world, "forensics" has come to mean the various procedures, many of them scientific in nature, used to answer questions of interest to the legal system—usually, to solve a crime. The Crime Scene Club has used many of these procedures in their cases. In this case, the procedures involved with skull reconstruction will help Lupe and Ken decipher a very different sort of crime case.

What Are Your Humerus and Your Ulna?

Your humerus and ulna are bones in your arm. The humerus is the long bone that connects your shoulder to your elbow. The ulna is one of two bones in the forearm (the radius is the other). The ulna connects with the humerus to form the elbow joint. The pointy part of your elbow is part of the ulna called the olecranon process.

What is NAGPRA?

NAGPRA stands for the Native American Graves Protection and Repatriation Act. It is a law originally passed in 1990 that protects Native American burials and associated sacred objects from being excavated or removed. The law also requires that any previously removed materials be returned (repatriated) to the proper tribal group.

Identification of Remains and Forensic Skull Reconstruction

One of the most important jobs assigned to a forensic anthropologist is to find the identity of skeletal remains. In modern criminal investigations, forensic anthropologists try to match the unidentified remains to missing person reports. Medical records, especially X-rays, can be matched to the remains to identify the individual. The anthropologist looks for unique marks on the bones, such as healed fractures, arthritis, or other abnormalities. Once an identity is suspected, the investigator may match the individual's skull to photographs in a process known as photo superimposition. A photograph of the individual is superimposed over a photograph of the skull to see if points on the face match the skull.

These techniques are useful in cases in which investigators have some sense of the victim's identity. In modern cases with no information or ancient cases like Una Vida woman, investigators have only the skeleton from which to gather identity information. Furthermore, in ancient cases, the skeleton is likely to consist of only a few fragments. Depending on where the pieces are from, they can still yield a lot of information about the individual. The archaeologist, like a forensic anthropologist, must read each bone carefully, looking for clues about the individual's life.

The skull is one of the most useful parts of the skeleton for identification purposes. The skull can be used for photo superimposition, but is also used in a process called facial reconstruction, facial approximation, or facial restoration. Facial reconstruction

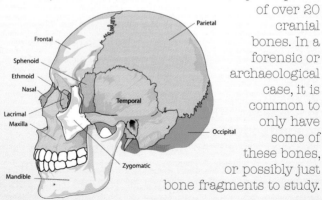

1.1 Many people think of the skull as a single unit, but the human skull is actually composed of over 20 cranial bones. In a forensic or archaeological case, it is common to only have some of these bones, or possibly just bone fragments to study.

combines art and science to sculpt a person's appearance using only characteristics of the skull and facial bones. Traditionally, facial reconstruction has been done using a skull cast and clay. In recent years there have been some advances in computer reconstruction programs, which Professor Tuwa suggests they will use to build a face for the Una Vida skeleton.

The Changing Woman Ceremony Today

A number of young Apache women today celebrate their first menstruation with the Apache Sunrise Ceremony. The ceremony can last anywhere from one to four days, and involves sacred rituals, prayers, dances, songs, and enactments. She gives food, gifts, and blessings to the community and receives from the community prayers and wishes for a prosperous, fruitful, and long life. The ceremony brings families and tribes together, strengthening their ties.

Running is also a part of the Sunrise Ceremony today, just as it was part of Naqali's ceremony. Running allows a young woman to show the physical strength and endurance she has achieved now that she is no longer a girl.

CHAPTER 2

Evidence List

Vocab Words

anorexia
nomadic

Deciphering the Evidence

When Lupe learns that the bones she is piecing together belonged to a female who suffered from malnutrition, she thinks of her personal struggle with *anorexia* over the past year. Anorexia is an eating disorder that occurs mainly among females that is characterized by an intense fear of gaining weight, self-starvation, and having a distorted body image.

Professor Tuwa explains to Lupe that members of *nomadic* tribes—those who wander from place to place—struggled for survival in ancient times.

Determining Sex from a Skeleton

One of the first questions in any forensic identification case is, "Is the individual male or female?" Forensic anthropologists must try to determine the sex of a skeleton using whatever bones are available. Some bones or techniques used commonly in sex determination include the pelvic girdle and the skull. If these elements are missing, the overall robusticity (height, size of muscle attachments) of the skeleton can be used to guess at the sex of the individual.

In adult skeletons, the bones of the pelvis are the preferred bones for sex determina-

Who Was Posada?

José Guadalupe Posada was a Mexican engraver and illustrator who lived from 1852 to 1913. He is best known for his cartoon-style illustrations of calaveras, which is the Spanish word for skulls. He often portrayed skeletons in humorous ways, such as the dancing cowboy and bargirl in the sketch that Lupe tapes to the wall.

What Is the Day of the Dead?

The Day of the Dead is a holiday observed mainly by Mexicans and Mexican-Americans over the course of two holy Catholic days: November 1 (All Saints' Day) and November 2 (All Souls' Day). El Día de los Muertos, as it is known in Spanish, is believed to be a time when the souls of the dead return to visit with their relatives. It is an occasion for remembering and honoring those who have departed this world, and also for celebrating the reunion of deceased relatives and their families with food, drink, and festivities.

tion. The female pelvis is shaped differently from the male pelvis mainly because of the requirements of childbirth. The female pelvis is wider and the hole formed by the two sides of the pelvis is larger; both of these traits allow an infant's head to pass through the pelvis during birth.

In addition to the difference of appearance of the whole pelvis, parts of each pelvic bone show characteristics that allow a forensic anthropologist to determine sex even if only part of the pelvis is present.

The skull is also used for determining sex. Overall size of the skull and of the muscle attachments are considered important, since males are generally larger and have bigger muscles, and therefore bigger muscle attachments, than females. Some specific parts of the skull that are considered are the mastoid process, the piece of bone that can be felt behind the ear. The mastoid process is generally larger and wider in males than in women. The occipital protuberance on the

2.1 Forensic scientists use the structural differences between the male and female pelvis to identify the sex of skeletal remains.

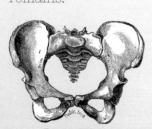

Female Pelvis

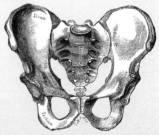

Male Pelvis

back of the skull is larger in men than in women. Also, men generally have squarer mandibles and chins, heavier brow ridges, and more pronounced bony ridges on the skull bones where the jaw muscles attach.

Dental Evidence

In many criminal investigations, forensic odontology plays an important role in helping to identify an unknown victim. Also called forensic dentistry, this science uses teeth to identify unknown individuals. Dental records and x-rays can be matched to a

What Is Tejano Music?

Tejano, or Texan, music is a type of music originating among Hispanics in Central and Southern Texas. It combines a mixture of styles ranging from folk, pop, and Latin to rock 'n roll, country, and rhythm and blues.

What Does Zygomatic Mean?

Zygomatic is the technical term for your cheekbone. You have two, one on either side of the face. The zygomatic bone forms the outside and bottom edge of the eye orbit, connects to the maxilla on the inside, and is linked to the temporal bone of the skull via a thin spur of bone called the zygomatic arch.

victim and used to determine identity. Bite marks left on a victim can be used to identify a suspect. Finally dental development and tooth wear can be used to determine age in children and adults.

In addition to their modern use in criminal investigations, teeth are important in many archaeological cases. This is partially because teeth are often preserved when other parts of the skeleton are not. Teeth also can give valuable information about an individual's age and health status. Professor Tuwa uses the molar from Una Vida Woman to determine that the young woman suffered from malnutrition and that she wasn't originally from Chaco Canyon. The malnutrition is apparent in her molar's thin enamel. Enamel also can indicate periods of sickness or high stress in the form of linear enamel hypoplasia, or horizontal lines of weaker enamel on the tooth. Professor Tuwa thinks Una Vida Woman came from an outlying tribe because her tooth doesn't show the pattern of wear that would be expected in a person eating stone ground corn meal like the tribes living within the Canyon. If Professor Tuwa was able to study the tooth using a stable isotope analysis, she might be able to determine the area where Una Vida Woman was born. However, like radiocarbon dating, stable isotope analysis is a destructive technique and is not always permitted on culturally sensitive remains.

CHAPTER 3

Evidence List

Vocab Words

exploits
taboo

Deciphering the Evidence

The hunters swap stories of their *exploits*, or heroic actions and deeds.

Naqali realizes that she has violated a *taboo* by speaking at a hunters' council. A taboo is something that is not allowed because of social custom.

More on Skull Reconstruction

A facial reconstruction is done by a forensic artist, who is also usually a forensic anthropologist with extensive knowledge of human anatomy. In a traditional reconstruction, the artist begins by making a cast of the skull. The cast is made to protect the original bones from damage and preserve them for future study. In the American Method, markers are placed in particular places on the face to indicate the correct tissue depth for each part of the face. Plastic balls are inserted into the eye sockets, and clay, representing muscles, is applied in strips to just barely cover and connect each of the markers.

People of the Great House

People of the Great House refers to the Anasazi, or Ancient Pueblo Peoples, whose culture thrived in the Chaco Canyon area of northwestern New Mexico between 900 and 1150 C.E. During this period, the Anasazi built a dozen or more gigantic buildings known as "Great Houses," as well as many other small pueblo houses and structures in outlying settlements. The Great Houses were huge, multistoried buildings, often containing several hundred rooms that served as living and storage quarters, food preparation and work areas, and spaces for community activities and ceremonies. The Anasazi left the Chaco Canyon region after 1300. According to historians, possible reasons for their departure include severe drought, loss of political power, and an attempt to find a location that provided better defense against enemies.

Once the "muscles" are completed, the surface is smoothed to resemble skin and aesthetic touches such as hair, eyebrows, and the shape of the nose are added. These characteristics cannot easily be determined from the shape of the skeletal bones. Instead, the artist will use other information to guess hair color and style; eye shape and color; and nose size and shape. These final touches can help make the face look more realistic, but if incorrect can also hinder the identification process. A slight difference in nose shape or a different hairstyle may be all that is necessary to identify the individual. These changes are difficult to make on a traditional reconstruction, but can be altered quickly and relatively easily on a computer facial reconstruction.

Computer reconstruction is done using many of the same underlying techniques as traditional reconstruction. A 3D image of the skull is created using a 3D scanner, through digital photography or by performing CT scans on the skull. The 3D image is then fed into a modeling program that contains a database of tissue depth information. The program then uses information entered about the probable sex, age and race of the individual to "sculpt" a face.

Computer reconstruction may be preferred because it removes artist bias and inconsistency of technique from the process. Given one skull, different artists would create multiple possible faces. A computer, on the other hand, should produce the same facial reconstruction every time, provided the same data is entered every time. Another benefit is the ease of changing features that was mentioned in the previous paragraph. Features can be quickly and easily altered on a computer reconstruction. Finally, computer reconstruction is a faster process than manual reconstruction, making it more useful in criminal investigations when time is of the essence.

CHAPTER 4

Evidence List

Vocab Words

medicine man   desecration
obsidian   indigenous
abhorrence

Deciphering the Evidence

Mr. Peshlaki was a painter and *medicine man*, a figure in Native American culture who seeks the help of the spirit world to heal others physically or spiritually.

The grooves on the arm bones contain tiny traces of *obsidian*, which is a dark volcanic glass formed by lava that has cooled quickly.

Professor Tuwa tells Lupe and Mr. Chesterton that Native American *abhorrence* for *desecration* of human remains has been a long-standing tradition. This means they have always felt a strong dislike or disapproval for anything that shows disrespect for something sacred, such as human remains.

The Native Americans Christopher Columbus encountered in the New World were *indigenous* to the land, meaning they were the original inhabitants.

Forensic Reconstruction

Working with an ancient skeleton is not much different that studying a modern skeleton as part of a criminal investigation. The forensic anthropologist begins with the same basic list of questions:

- Are the bones human or nonhuman?
- What was the age of the individual at the time of death?
- Is the individual male or female?
- What was the ethnic affiliation of the individual?
- What was the individual's stature?
- What are the individual's unique characteristics?
- What caused the individual to die?

When piecing together the identity of a modern or an ancient skeleton, the forensic anthropologist must consider all the evidence,

4.1 When skeletal remains are discovered, forensic anthropologists carefully lay out the bones of each individual to do inventory on which bones are present before doing any closer study of the bones themselves.

even that which is not obvious right away. Healed injuries, changes caused by illness, weapon marks, and post mortem effects like rodent gnaw marks or excavation damage all may show as tiny marks. In order to interpret the meaning of these marks, a microscope may be needed. When Professor Tuwa examines the ends of the humerus and ulna under a microscope she finds strange cut marks with bits of obsidian in them. The marks are similar to butchering marks seen on the bones of animals killed for food. Mr. Chesterton has also seen similar marks in a modern criminal case involving cannibalism.

There is debate among Southwestern archaeologists about whether or not cannibalism was practiced among the ancestors of the Hopi and Zuni. Some archaeologists, including Christy Turner from Arizona State University, believe that many Chaco Canyon bones do show evidence of cannibalism. Turner looks for six forensic identifiers of cannibalism among the Ancestral Puebloan's bones: burning (especially on the skull), scrapes made by an anvil, cuts on the ends of long bones, bones broken for marrow, bone ends that are polished from boiling in a ceramic pot (pot polish), and a lack of vertebrae. Other archaeologists, like Professor Tuwa, think that these marks are signs of ritual cleaning prior to burial, rather than cannibalism. She comes to this conclusion by drawing on her extensive knowledge of modern Hopi and Zuni cultural beliefs about respecting the dead.

CHAPTER 5

Evidence List

Vocab Words

talisman   sensational
fetish   expertise
symmetry

Deciphering the Evidence

Along with her knife, Naqali brings a *talisman* given to her by her mother—a finely beaded purse. A talisman is an object that is believed to offer protection and bring good fortune; it is a type of good-luck charm.

Inside Naqali's sacred pouch is a rainbow-colored shell and a turquoise bear *fetish*. A fetish is an object believed to have magical powers to protect and help its owner.

Professor Tuwa believes that the missing piece of skull was surgically removed because of the *symmetry*—the regularity or similarity—of the cuts.

According to the professor, museums try to make money by being *sensational*, or creating an excited reaction in people through the use of exaggerated or startling details.

Despite the professor's *expertise*, Lupe wonders if her skill and knowledge in the field of archaeology can ultimately explain what really happened to Una Vida Woman.

Who Were the Aztecs?

The Aztecs were a Native American tribe who are believed to have migrated south from Aztlan, their homeland in the remote areas of northern Mexico to settle in central Mexico in the 13th century. They built a great empire in the 15th century that included cities, pyramids, and temples, as well as a government, a trading network, and an advanced agricultural economy. The Aztec empire was destroyed in 1521 by Spanish soldiers led by Hernàndo Cortés.

What Are Chert and Obsidian?

Chert, sometimes called flint, is a sedimentary rock composed of microscopic quartz crystals. Chert can range in color from light gray to shades of red, yellow and dark gray. Obsidian is an igneous, or volcanic, rock that is formed when lava comes into contact with water. Obsidian has a dark, shiny, glass-like appearance. Both obsidian and chert were commonly used by ancient people to make sharp blades, projectile points, and other stone tools.

Who Were the Conquistadors

The term *conquistadors* is most often used to refer to the Spanish conquerors who defeated Indian civilizations in Mexico and the Americas in the sixteenth century.

Forensic Reconstruction

Bone is a living tissue that is sensitive to changes in health and nutrition status. Depending on the type of disease or stress, extra bone tissue may develop or bones may get weaker and thinner. Injuries to bone are also recorded in unique ways depending on the cause, and when the injuries occurred. Professor Tuwa can tell when the missing piece of skull was removed because a healed injury that happened while the person was alive (antemortem injury) will look different from an injury that occurred at or around the time of death (perimortem injury). Both types of injuries will look very different from postmortem damage to the skeleton. Healed injuries have smooth, rounded edges where the bone has started to remodel. Perimortem injuries show no signs of healing, but do show damage consistent with the fact that the bone was still living and soft when the injury occurred. Also, because the bone was broken prior to being buried, the inside edges of the break will be stained the same color as the outside of the bone. Postmortem damage, perhaps caused by a shovel during excavation of the remains, will show sharp jagged edges that are much lighter in color than the outside of the bone.

An individual's age is also recorded in their skeleton. Aging techniques differ between adults and subadults (children). Subadults can be aged relatively accurately to within a couple of years based on the fusion of the epiphyses at different points in the body. Epiphyses are the unattached ends of long bones that only fuse after growth is complete. Different epiphyses fuse at different ages. Both ends of the humerus fuse between the ages of 10 and 15 in women, while the ulnar ends fuse a bit later—between the ages of 17 and 20. Skull sutures can also be used for aging, though their usefulness is more debatable. Generally, cranial sutures remain relatively open prior to the age of 30, so by looking at Una Vida Woman's, Professor Tuwa is only able to determine that she must be younger than thirty years old.

Una Vida Woman's jaws and teeth can give a lot of information about her age. In fact, because dental development and eruption have regular times, and because teeth are the most commonly found skeletal remains in forensic and archaeological cases, dental development is the most commonly used aging technique for subadult remains. The second molars complete eruption between about 11-15 years of age. After this,

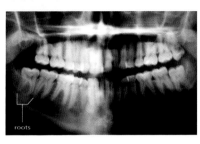

5.1 To study the dental development of Una Vida woman, Professor Tuwa would take an x-ray like this one. The x-ray shows the roots of the teeth, allowing a more accurate assessment of age based on dental development.

in the late teenage years, the third molars, or wisdom teeth may or may not appear. If Una Vida Woman has third molars, Professor Tuwa could age her to >15 years. If she does not have third molars, Professor Tuwa will look to the wear on her teeth to determine her age. By comparing the wear patterns on Una Vida Woman's teeth to dental wear charts for her time period and population, Professor Tuwa can determine that she must be between 12 and 18 years of age. Professor Tuwa then combines all the age ranges from the different aging techniques, and takes the overlapping ranges to come to her final conclusion that Una Vida Woman was a teenager, possibly a bit younger than Lupe.

CHAPTER 6

Evidence List

Vocab Words

cairn
intimidating

Deciphering the Evidence

After the hunter passes into the spirit world, Naqali covers his body with a simple *cairn*. A cairn is a pile of rocks built to memorialize the dead.

Naqali finds the outlying settlement of the Great House People to be *intimidating*. Their dwellings, dress, tools, and weapons are superior to those of her own tribe, causing her to feel inadequate or afraid.

Facial Reconstruction Case File

Giving a Face to King Tut

In 2005, three different forensic artist teams were given the task of reconstructing Tutankhamun's face. Dr. Zahi Hawass, Secretary General of Egypt's Supreme Council of Antiquities, led the project. The first step in the experiment involved taking a CT scan of the mummy. The scan was carefully done to avoid damaging the fragile pharaoh. Over 1,700 images were taken during the scan; these were used to created 3-D models.

The CT scan information was given to three forensic teams: an American team, a French team, and an Egyptian team. The American and French teams were also given a plastic model of the skull, while the Egyptian team made its own model. Both the Egyptian and French teams knew that they were working with King Tut, but the American team was working blind. All three teams used traditional modeling techniques—determining racial type and then applying clay muscles to the model. Each team then applied skin and other features to make the reconstruction look more realistic. The end results revealed three models that were nearly identical in the shape of the face, size and setting of the eyes, and the basic proportions of the skull. The shape of the ears and the end of the nose varied between all three teams. Overall, however, Dr. Hawass thought that all three of the reconstructions were very similar to a famous image of Tutankhamun as a child. The experiment was viewed as a success in showing that facial reconstruction can be a useful tool for revealing faces from the past.

6.1 The face of Tutankhamun as reconstructed by the team of French forensic scientists.

CHAPTER 7

Evidence List

Vocab Words

musculature
collagen
Hogan
stereotype

Deciphering the Evidence

Professor Tuwa uses a computer program to create the *musculature* over the image of the skull. Musculature means the muscles of all or part of a body.

Professor Tuwa adds thin lips to the reconstructed head because malnourishment would have decreased the amount of *collagen* in the girl's body. Collagen is the main protein in our bodies, and is found in skin, bones, tendons, cartilage, and ligaments.

Stanley Peshlaki lived in a traditional Navajo Indian home made of logs and mud called a *Hogan*.

Mr. Peshlaki is bothered by the fact that people *stereotype* Native art. To stereotype something is to suggest that everything in the same category has the same characteristics.

Forensic Reconstruction

CAT Scans

A computerized axial tomography scan, more commonly called a CAT or CT scan, is a procedure that takes images of the inside of the body. A conventional X-ray machine takes a 2D picture of one part of the body. A CT scan, on the other hand, produces cross sectional images that look like slices of the body. The CT scanning machine is an X-ray unit that rotates around the entire body and takes pictures from every angle. These pictures are then sent to a computer and combined to form cross-sectional scans of the whole body. While an X-ray shows overlapping outlines of bones and other organs, a CT scan shows the internal anatomy of all the organs. CT scans are useful for skeletal reconstruction for this reason—they reveal details of the bones, as well as the muscle and fat tissue depths in every location on the body.

7.1 A technician positioning a young patient for a CT scan.

Evidence List

Vocab Words

escarpment   replicated
prevail   clarify
patronize

Deciphering the Evidence

Trying to find a way into one of the dwellings that make up The Great House, Naqali spies a ledge and begins to climb the rocky *escarpment*. An escarpment is a steep slope or long cliff often caused by erosion.

Weyaka assures Naqali that they will *prevail* over the guards, who suspect nothing and are outnumbered. Prevail means to triumph or be victorious over.

When Mr. Chesterton tells Lupe that she's stressed because she's been through a lot, she feels he is treating her in a condescending manner, and tells him not to *patronize* her.

As a science teacher, Mr. Chesterton believes in things that can be *replicated*, which means reproduced or repeated.

Mr. Chesterton tells Lupe that he is trying to help her *clarify* her thoughts. To clarify is to make clear or free of confusion.

132

What Is a Spear-Thrower?

A spear-thrower, also called an atlatl, is a tool that allows a hunter or warrior to throw a spear or dart with greater speed. A spear-thrower is a straight stick with a handle at one end and a curved cup at the other in which the end of the spear rests. As the thrower pulls the arm forward while throwing, the leverage provided by the atlatl projects a spear much faster and farther than it could be thrown by an arm alone.

The Scientific Method

The scientific method is a process that scientists use to study the world. It involves the use of systematic observations, hypotheses, experimentation and analysis to come to any conclusions. The scientific method is built on the idea that to be reliable and accurate any information must be gained by following the same set of steps. The steps of the scientific method are:

- Ask a question.
- Do background research.
- Develop a hypothesis.
- Test the hypothesis with an experiment; then carefully record experiment process and results.
- Analyze the experiment results and develop new hypothesis if necessary.

133

- Report the results.
- Retest (usually done by other scientists).

The final step in the process is actually the most important. If the scientific method was followed correctly, another scientist should be able to reproduce the same results by following the same steps. This is why Mr. Chesterton is so against Lupe's ghost hypothesis. As he says, he believes in things he can weigh, test and replicate—things that he can see and prove with the scientific method.

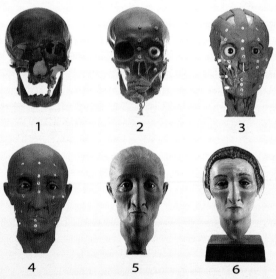

8.1 This image exhibits the progression from skull to fully completed facial reconstruction of a woman from the 18th century in Albany, NY. Except for the final, artistic interpretation of her coloring and hair, the reconstruction uses scientific methods and measurements so that another forensic artist could reproduce the same face.

134

CHAPTER 9

Evidence List

Vocab Words

crone
destiny
plaintive
cadence

Deciphering the Evidence

As she awaits her fate, Naqali closes her eyes and in her mind hears the words of the old *crone*, Sage Woman. Crone means withered old woman.

When she thinks about how the People will survive because of her act of bravery, Naqali realizes she has fulfilled her *destiny*. A person's destiny is the life purpose or fate that he or she was meant to have.

At the site of the grave for Una Vida Woman's remains, Mr. Peshlaki sang in a *plaintive* tone, expressing sorrow for her through his song.

While he sang, Mr. Peshlaki tapped his leg in a steady *cadence* or beat.

Wrapping Up CSC #6

This case seemed different from the other Crime Scene Club cases in many ways. The site was not a modern crime scene, but an archaeological dig; the victim was only represented by a few pieces of a skeleton; and there was no clear crime case to solve. Even though the individual was a prehistoric skeleton from an archaeological site, however, Lupe was able to learn many skills applicable to a modern forensic case. In fact, the techniques applied to the archaeological remains were all the same techniques that would be applied in a modern forensic identification case. At the end of the case, however, there is no identification. They have a picture of a face, but no name. They learned little about Una Vida Woman's life and less about why she died.

Lupe is especially frustrated by the lack of answers; after all, she has been used to successfully solving crimes. At the end of each case, a bad guy is caught and the victim is vindicated. Justice is done. Professor Tuwa understands Lupe's frustration, but explains that with archaeological cases, there are almost always more questions than answers. Techniques like facial reconstruction may seem like magic, but in reality they are imperfect. The truth is, plenty of modern criminal cases leave questions unanswered as well. Many facial reconstructions are done with the goal of identifying a "John Doe," but more often than not, no one recognizes the face and the case goes unsolved. In this case, the goal of studying the bones was identification for tribal affiliation to allow for repatriation and proper burial. Thanks to Lupe, Professor Tuwa and the facial reconstruction, this goal was successfully attained. Lupe should be happy: Naqali is finally at peace and back with her people.

FURTHER READING

Bass, Bill. 2003. *Death's Acre: Inside the Legendary Forensic Lab-Where the Dead do Tell Tales.* New York: G. P. Putnam's Sons.

Craig, Emily. 2004. *Teasing Secrets from the Dead. My Investigations at America's Most Infamous Crime Scenes.* New York, NY: Crown Publishers

Ferllini, Roxana. 2002. *Silent Witness. How Forensic Anthropology is Used to Solve the World's Toughest Crimes.* Buffalo, NY: Firefly Books

Innes, Brian. 2006. *Forensic Science.* Philadelphia, PA: Mason Crest Publishers.

Jackson, Donna M. 1996. *The Bone Detectives: How Forensic Anthropologists Solve Crimes and Uncover Mysteries of the Dead.* New York: Little, Brown and Company.

Manhein, Mary H. 1999. *The Bone Lady: Life as a Forensic Anthropologist.* Baton Rouge: Louisiana State University Press.

Ubelaker, Douglas and Henry Scammell. 2000. *Bones: A Forensic Detective's Casebook.* New York: Harper Collins.

FOR MORE INFORMATION

American Academy of Forensic Sciences. www.aafs.org

Ancient Pueblo Peoples
www.blm.gov/co/st/en/fo/ahc/who_were_the_anasazi.html

Facial Reconstruction
www.forensicartist.com/reconstruction.html

FBI Unravels the Stories Skulls Tell by Dina Temple-Raston. http://www.npr.org/templates/story/story.php?storyId=18481926

How Stuff Works, "How Crime Scene Investigation Works," www.howstuffworks.com/csi.htm

New York Cultural Resource Survey Program
www.nysm.nysed.gov/research/anthropology/crsp/arccrsppearlstfacial.html

Skeletal Remains Identification by Facial Reconstruction
www.fbi.gov/hq/lab/fsc/backissu/jan2001/phillips.htm

BIBLIOGRAPHY

Bahn, Paul G. 2003. *Written in Bones: How Human Remains Unlock the Secrets of the Dead.* Buffalo, NY: Firefly Books

Genge, N. E. 2002. *The Forensic Casebook.* New York: Ballantine Books.

Hawass, Dr. Zahi. "Tutankhamun Facial Reconstruction." www.guardians.net/hawass/Press_Release_05-05_Tut_Reconstruction.htm

Lyle, D.P. 2004. *Forensics for Dummies.* Indianapolis, IN: Wiley Publishing Inc.

Ortner, Donald J. *Identification of Pathological Conditions in Human Skeletal Remains, Second Edition.* San Diego, CA: Academic Press, 2003.

Owen, David. 2000. *Hidden Evidence. Forty True Crimes and How Forensic Science Helped Solved Them.* Buffalo, NY: Firefly Books

Steadman, Dawnie W. *Hard Evidence: Case Studies in Forensic Anthropology.* Upper Saddle River, NJ: Prentice Hall.

Wecht, Cyril H. 2004. *Crime Scene Investigation.* Pleasantville, NY: The Reader's Digest Association, Inc.

White, Tim. *Human Osteology, Second Edition.* San Diego, CA: Academic Press, 2000.

INDEX

PICTURE CREDITS

BIOGRAPHIES

Author

Kenneth McIntosh is a freelance writer and college instructor who lives in beautiful Flagstaff, Arizona (while CSC is fictional, Flagstaff is definitely real). He has enjoyed crime fiction—from Sherlock Holmes to CSI and Bones—and is thankful for the opportunity to create his own detective stories. Now, if he could only find his car keys . . .

Ken would like to thank the following people:
Tom Oliver, who invented the title 'Crime Scene Club' on a tram en route to the Getty Museum, and cooked up the best plots while we sat at his Tiki bar . . . Mr. Levin's Creative Writing students at the Flagstaff Arts and Leadership Academy, *who vetted the books . . . Rob and Jenny Mullen and Victor Viera, my Writer's Group, who shared their lives and invaluable insights . . . My recently deceased father, Dr. A Vern McIntosh, who taught me when I was a child to love written words. This series could not have happened without all of you.*

Series Consultant

Carla Miller Noziglia is Senior Forensic Advisor, Tanzania, East Africa, for the U.S. Department of Justice, International Criminal Investigative Training Assistant Program. A Fellow of the American Academy of Forensic Sciences her work has earned her many honors and commendations, including Distinguished Fellow from the American Academy of Forensic Sciences (2003) and the Paul L.

Kirk Award from the American Academy of Forensic Sciences Criminalistics Section. Ms. Noziglia's publications include *The Real Crime Lab* (coeditor, 2005), *So You Want to be a Forensic Scientist* (coeditor 2003), and contributions to *Drug Facilitated Sexual Assault* (2001), *Convicted by Juries, Exonerated by Science: Case Studies in the Use of DNA* (1996), and the *Journal of Police Science* (1989).

Illustrator

Justin Miller first discovered art while growing up in Gorham, ME. He developed an interest in the intersection between science and art at the University of New Hampshire while studying studio art and archaeology. He applies both degrees in his job at the Public Archaeology Facility at Binghamton University. He also enjoys playing soccer, hiking, and following English Premier League football.